THE
DEBUTANTE
(AND THE BOMB FACTORY)

Cover and Interior Design: Lauren Vajda, Verso Design, *www.versodesign.co*
Cover photography: Jonathan Knowles via Getty Images

Published by Debutante Press LLC
(a Massachusetts limited liability company)
Chestnut Hill, MA

First paperback edition, December, 2020

ISBN 978-1-7363627-1-6

THE DEBUTANTE

(AND THE BOMB FACTORY)

A NOVEL BY
JONATHAN CANTER

DEBUTANTE PRESS LLC
CHESTNUT HILL, MA

DISCLAIMER

THIS IS A WORK OF FICTION

IT IS A WORK OF FICTION (it could be called a fictional love story) that plays out against a background of historical events—including historical events pertaining to opposition to the War in Vietnam, and to activities of the Weathermen, a/k/a the Weather Underground, in the 1960s and after. Notwithstanding the background of historical events, the names, characters, incidents and dialogue which are included in the story are either the product of the author's imagination or are used fictitiously, and any resemblance in the story to actual persons living or dead is coincidental and is not intended to refer to any actual persons, except that certain actual persons whose names are part of the historical record of the times are referred to in connection with recitation of the historical record.

Without limiting the foregoing, the narrator is fictional, and is not the author. The narrator has his own mind, and any objectionable thinking of the narrator is not necessarily shared by the author.

PART I

"GOOD AFTERNOON, CLASS," I SAID FROM MY LECTERN. I fussed with my papers and cleared my throat. I gave a quick, professorial scan to the room, looking for oddities, like a new face, or a new hair arrangement, or a bomb. My persona, the one I've developed over the past many years of teaching history at Wesleyan University in Connecticut, is of a wizened, battle-scarred academic. My belly pushes over my belt. My beard is frizzy. My eyes are sad, from reading too many sad books, and too many ridiculous term-papers.

My best friend is my brown tweed jacket. I've worn him through chalk smears, wine spills, snow falls, and our share of blue nights spent sleeping with the dog. His side pockets are distended from being stuffed with water bottles and magazines. He could use some care and love. He's past his prime and sort of a mess, like me.

The day was a cold one, at the end of January. The day's light was already fading, and it would be black as night before the end of class, which is one of my favorite situations—the end of a winter's day—except that I prefer to experience it with a friendly Scotch or two at the Faculty Club, and let the sealing effect of the darkness work in tandem with the creep of intoxication.

Yes, I say, to that moment of relief at the far end of my day.

Yes, I have regrets.

A couple of my students murmured good afternoons back at me. Some were too absorbed in last minute texting to yield the floor. Some had already assumed a posture of indifference, heads turned to the tall windows on the side, young minds gone fishing.

"We'll finish with the Weathermen...the Weather Underground... today...and..."

A hand shot up in the first row. Michelle, a girl with dark ringlets, peering over the top of her MacBook.

"Yes?"

"Do we have to remember who was sleeping with who..."

"Whom..." Sometimes I can't help myself.

"...because you made a big deal of the fact that the guy whose girl-friend was blown up in the townhouse hooked up with the girl who used to sleep with..."

"My point was...Who remembers my point?"

Pause.

A hand in the back.

"Yes, Gisele," I said. She wore a puffy parka despite the gusts of hot air that swirled around the room and prompted others to strip down to T-shirts, suggesting she could use a warm-up hug, but that's not my business.

"Professor," Gisele said, "you were saying that the Weathermen were first-most a social organization, sort of like a hippie commune, and they all slept with each other because they had freed themselves from bourgeois conventions..."

"Okay, but...yes," I said to another hand in the air, belonging to my reliable star, Larry.

"I took your attention to whom they were sleeping with as a comment on the lark they were living. They were kids playing at being revolutionaries. They weren't serious political people, even when they were smashing windshields with baseball bats..."

"Yes, Larry. I think that's correct. They weren't serious..."

"What was that?" asked Michelle, from the front row.

An hour later I glanced to my watch and confirmed the *tempus fugit* message being transmitted up the grid from my feet to my knees to my hips. I'm a stand-up teacher, but not as spry as I used to be. I creak toward the end of a session. I nodded to my class: *you are free to go.*

They rose as one and shuffled to the exit seemingly cool and blasé notwithstanding the experiential opportunities that dot each day of late adolescence, not that I'm jealous. I gathered my papers and wiped off my chalky hands on my loyal tweed. *Not a bad session. We got into the decision-making—should I make bombs today or finish my application to law school? We did some psychoanalysis—my dad's thick as stone, my mom's a ditz, and I'm living large on the barricades...We...*

"Professor Cox," said Louisa, who hadn't said two words the whole semester. I put her in the cute and stylish category, with things going on other than the academics. She curled from the exiting pack and approached me at the lectern.

"Yes."

"My aunt was in the Days of Rage, in Chicago."

"No kidding..." This was exciting information for me. "Did she run through the streets?"

"She did. She still has her helmet."

"Was she arrested?"

"No. She says she was quick and evasive..."

"Good for her...What does she do now?"

"She's a lawyer..."

"Really. Very interesting. What's her name?"

"Aunt Liz...I MEAN Elizabeth Caruso."

"Caruso? I don't remember any..."

"Oh, her maiden name was Seaver. Elizabeth Seaver.[1]

"Yes, Elizabeth Seaver. Went to Bryn Mawr. Grew up outside of Boston..."

"How do you know that?"

"I'm a student of the Weathermen. I'm writing a book..."

So, on an unlovely Saturday two weeks later as winter dragged his old bones through the slush, and the sun extended her vacation in

---

[1] "Elizabeth Seaver Caruso" is not her real name. I made it up, because I'm pretty sure she doesn't want her real name dragged into the Weatherman spotlight at this late date. And, at the risk of getting ahead of myself in this narrative, she already hates me enough, so why make it worse?

Florida, I rang Elizabeth Seaver Caruso's bell at her condominium on Beacon Street in Boston's Back Bay. Beacon Street—for those of you from elsewhere—is the last street before the Charles River if you're walking north in the direction of Cambridge from Commonwealth Avenue. The housing stock is not as grand on Beacon as it is on Commonwealth, except that if you're lucky enough to live on the river side of Beacon you might have a panoramic view that is basically unique and priceless. The Esplanade, the domes of Harvard, the route ridden by Paul Revere, and on a clear day New Hampshire. My mother and I lived on the *non*-river side in my teen-age years.

I had called Ms. Caruso in advance to explain myself, that her niece was in my class and suggested I call, that I'm writing a book about the Weathermen, that I wanted to interview as many former Weathermen as possible, such as herself. She was on the cool side of lukewarm to my request. She said it was not her practice to share her past with strangers. Besides, what good does it do to look back? But in the end, she allowed me a meeting.

She buzzed me in and was waiting on the third-floor landing when I emerged from the elevator. Much older than her Bryn Mawr pictures, obviously, but I recognized her plain and wholesome good looks, which is one of the consistent trademarks of a Weather Woman. They had good teeth, good dexterity, and probably could have been good country club tennis players if things had played out differently.

"Come in, Professor Cox," she said. She gave me a professional handshake—one quick, firm pump—and took my coat which she draped over the back of a foyer chair and pointed at my galoshes which I took off and left on a mat near my coat. She glided me to a cozy parlor overlooking the river. Embers glowed in an old-fangled fireplace.

"Call me Liz," she said.

"Call me Linc,"[2] I said.

She wore a turtleneck and zipper vest, above jeans and slippers.

---

2 "Lincoln Cox" is my *nom de plume*. Sounds to me like a person of stature, honor and good breeding. An aspirational name.

She was slender. Her hair was chopped short, and held in place with a barrette, old girl style. She directed me to the central chair, with the best view of the river. She sat herself on the couch to the other side of the fire, with a view of me. She reached for the poker and stabbed the main log in the belly.

"You know," she said, "there's been so much noise recently about the Weathermen, that I'm thinking about going underground again to get away from it…"

"The Ayers' thing," I said. "His relation to Obama got a lot of people revved up…"

"No doubt that. But I feel a general awakening of attention…"

"A reunion is planned…"

"For Chicago. On the anniversary of the Days of Rage. I don't know how many people will go. A lot of us outgrew it…"

"…Some are still in jail…"

"…Or underground…"

"…Or feeling bitter and betrayed…"

"…Yes, all that…," she said, and sighed for the old days, or what-ever. She seemed quite pleasant and genuine. "My niece says she enjoys your class very much…"

"…Oh, I'm pleased to hear that. It's a lively class. The Vietnam Era. Tonkin Gulf. Daniel Ellsberg. Hippies, for goodness sakes…"

"…You're writing a book?"

"…Sort of a where-are-they-now compendium, updating the bios of Weathermen, and some fellow travelers. Not just headline names—Ayers, Boudin, Dohrn—but also the rank and file, the foot soldiers, the footnote people. I'm looking for what happened to the revolutionary zeal, for what lessons we can learn from this slice of countercultural Americana…"

"…Have you spoken to many?"

"…A few."

"…They're willing to speak?"

"…Some yes. Some no. Some love to dig it up and shake it out. Some hate it and want to keep it buried. A mixed bag…"

She curled her legs under her, kitten like. She kept hold of her poker, wagging it. Her gaze drifted past me, to the middle distance, which I took to be a sign that she was dredging up the old stuff, which I wanted to encourage. I tried not to be too pushy in these interviews. I realized there was often a pot of emotions stewing below the surface— pride, guilt, horror, regret about bombs—and that they're more likely to spill it out if they feel at ease, like they're talking to an easy-going contemporary. As opposed to an FBI agent, for example. So I leaned back into my comfortable chair, and took a look at the river flowing by on its way to the sea, more black than blue, more tar than water, as grim a river as ever I've seen, and counted my Mississippis, all the way to Seven Mississippi when she broke the silence.

"Professor Cox..."

"...Linc, please...or Lincoln, but most folks call me Linc."

"...Linc, what got you so interested in the Weathermen?"

"...I'm a historian...It's interesting historical material...I..."

"...You're my age, right?"

"...Right."

"...College in the late Sixties?"

"...Right."

"...What did you think about the war?"

"...I was anti-war, big-time."

"...Demonstrations?"

"...Yes."

"...On campus?"

"...Yes."

"...D.C.?"

"...Yes. The Spring Mobilization and..."

"...SDS?"

"...No. I wasn't...but I knew SDS guys..."

"...Did you know Weathermen?"

"...Yes, some..."

"...Who?"

"...Oh a few...I was a repor...ah, let me ask you a question. What kind of lawyer are you? It feels like you're a litigator..."

"...I litigate, and other things. I'm doing entertainment packages these days..."

"...Was the Weathermen stuff a problem for you when you applied to the bar?"

"...Fortunately not. I don't have a record. I was almost arrested, but wasn't. I was a fast runner..."

"...You went underground?"

"...Briefly, as a precaution."

"...Incriminating photographs?"

"...It's been forty years and none have shown up...I think I'm in the clear."

"...Regrets?"

"...Regarding?"

"...Getting involved with the Weathermen?"

"...What made sense then is not the same as what makes sense today...I..."

Her telephone rang.

Yes," she said into it, "I know who you are..."

She listened.

I kept my ears on her, but to appear less intrusive I shifted my gaze back to the non-shimmering river, with ice mounting around the bridge abutments. No rowers or gulls today, hearty as each might be. I heard her murmur assents into her phone. "Yes...mmmm...yes...." In the corner of my eye I saw unease cross her face, and glares dart toward me. I was involved in this telephone call.

"Thanks for calling," she said, and disconnected.

To me she said, "Professor Lincoln Cox, you have a reputation."

"What do you mean?"

"I hear that..."

"...Who called?"

"...you are a rat..."

✹

I COME WITH BAGGAGE. Who doesn't? To begin, and please forgive me, but once I was in love. Sometimes when I think about her today, the love sensation comes back as a recognizable throb, not unlike the return of a favorite taste or aroma, or hallucination.

She—Samantha Victor[3]—was a senior at a private girl's school when I was a freshman at college.[4]

I met her at a debutante cotillion—a high-class mixer—at a big old mansion on a hill with lawns rolling down to the Atlantic Ocean, on a balmy evening in early September, 1966, at the start of my freshman year, at the debut of my own life, with a live orchestra and an open bar, and flowers and lanterns everywhere. I think they imported birds to sing.

Samantha was a deb, along with a dozen other girls of her social circle. Her father, may he rest in peace although he hated me, was an important banker of the era, whose bank has long since been cannibalized by guys from New York. Her mother was a great beauty and socialite of the 1950s and into the 1960s, but descended to serious drinking in the 1970s, and died under unfortunate circumstances, likely an overdose, arguably quickened by the crazy path chosen by her only child. May her mother also rest in peace, although she hated me more than her husband. They both erroneously thought I was responsible for turning Samantha to radical politics.

I was invited to the ball on the strength of my pedigree and school ties, i.e., by then my father was dead and my family—my mother and I—exiled from the moneyed classes, getting by on fumes and manners. Once we built railroads, as they say.

Samantha arrived to the front door of the mansion in a horse-drawn carriage, festooned with flowers, on the arm of her beaming father. She wore a yellow (yellow!) ball gown, of filmy chiffon and

---

3 I changed Samantha's last name too.

4 Harvard College, but that name brand is not really relevant to this accounting. Or is it? I take it as a stand-in for any elite all-purpose university in the northeast whose campus was likewise embroiled by radical politics in the 1960s.

other ethereal components. She was altogether lovely, in the mold of many future Weather Women. Good posture, lithe body movement, winning smile, matching bouquet, and in her particular case, freckles.

I connived for an hour on how best to approach her, and I wasn't the only one. A pack of preppy guys in tailored dinner jackets and patent leather pumps had picked up her scent. You know these guys—or maybe you don't, and for all I know maybe they don't exist anymore, except that I think they tend to regenerate each generation as the dinner jackets get passed down provided the trust funds are wisely invested and the alcohol doesn't eliminate them too early. They're eligible, even though some are very dense, and can play golf and squash with their fathers-in-law.

I fit into the pack in those days, externally anyways—I had thick hair, a thin waist, a clear complexion, and a new-looking plaid cummerbund—but internally I wasn't a good pack guy anymore, more like a lone wolf. I was developing symptoms of class bitterness.

I was also worrying about the draft. LBJ doubled troop levels each quarter, and haplessly looked for light at the end of his tunnel. That was his big expression, a light at the end of the tunnel, a sign that victory in the Vietnam War was in sight. Meanwhile, it just got darker and darker for everybody. Lyndon—may he too rest in peace, or at least not too uncomfortably—never realized how trapped he was. The more troops he sent, the more distant his victory drifted. His only way out was to acknowledge his mistake and order a retreat, but he had the big man syndrome and couldn't do that, which obliged me to focus my attention on my goal of not dying young and purposelessly in a rice paddy.

I was also on my way to parting company from God. The God stuff seemed so juvenile to me, and still does, even though odd episodes in my life have insinuated the unnerving possibility of divine intervention. One was an hour-long intervention at the craps tables at Mandalay Bay in Vegas in the winter of 2004, and another was this time at the deb ball when I strolled to the veranda for a smoke and a good look at the starry sky and found Samantha standing there ahead of me. With tears flowing from her eyes from a big fight she'd just had with her mother, and no handkerchief until I arrived and offered mine.

Oh God, to kiss her lips under the stars as tears continued to roll down her cheeks. Chanel No. 5, borrowed from her mother, filled the air. I should have died then.

Mr. and Mrs. Victor came to hate me, but not at first. They didn't object to football games in the fall, or plays in the winter, or walks along the river in the springtime, all of which were within the margins of traditional dating patterns, and might have had a fair chance of leading to traditional connubial bliss, except that by the springtime of 1967 marijuana was in the air, everywhere. Traditional values were going up in smoke. Life was strumming a Bob Dylan song.

When the Victors found marijuana in Samantha's pockets—again, not my doing— that's when they started to hate me. Since then I've wondered where the hell did all the marijuana come from? The marijuana in her pants, and the marijuana in every pipe, joint and brownie from Cambridge to California. Was it collected and stored in some huge warehouse by a prescient capitalist waiting for the boom? Did some marketing genius lay down the plan to distribute it from campus to campus, dorm to dorm, bunk to bunk, mouth to mouth? How do you go from no marijuana to pandemic proportions in the wink of an eye? It wouldn't surprise me if it was a Cold War conspiracy.

Marijuana, Vietnam War, *rock and roll!* Those were the days.

Mr. Victor, Samantha's dad, didn't necessarily love the war, but he sure as hell hated the anti-war, and the disorder and degeneracy it fomented. The last time I saw him, in August 1968, on the eve of the Democratic National Convention, which his daughter was planning to attend and disrupt, he was trying to kill me with her baseball bat.

✳

"A RAT?" I said to Elizabeth Seaver Caruso.

"Please leave," she said to me.

"I..."

"Please leave." She uncurled from the couch and stood straight. She still waved the poker, one of those yard-long brass jobs with a sharp point, resembling a sword.

"Who called?"

She growled at me like a provoked dog.

I didn't have the means or wit to turn her around. I nodded obsequiously and backed out of the cozy room with the river view and kept backing out until I had my coat and galoshes in hand and the elevator took me away.

I reached the street unnerved, assuming that someone—some crazy old Weatherman with an axe to grind—knew I was with her and called because I was with her, which meant he was tracking me, and cared enough to call to say bad things about me, and was now possibly hiding behind that mail box or sitting in the white van with tinted windows across the street.

"Shit, not this again," I said to myself. I pulled my wool hat down low and made a zig-zag dash for my car. On a cold day I was sweating like a pig.

I reached my car.

I scanned the street while I jiggered with my door lock. No obvious followers, no interested spectators, no wild-eyed old Weatherman with an axe. Just a quiet, slushy street.

I swung the door open and climbed in. I turned my ignition key, taking comfort from the fact that as far as I knew car bombs had not previously been part of Weatherman *modus operandi*. There was a *vrooom*, and not a *kaboom*, to my relief. I breathed out, and let the engine run for a few minutes, until heat rose and my sweating lowered, and my pounding heart settled back into its cavity.

I had another interview scheduled, at the Casablanca Bar in Harvard Square. I didn't know my interviewee. I didn't know his "agent" who had arranged the interview. I only knew, or was told, that my interviewee's *nom de guerre* was Tim, that he'd be wearing a red bandana, and that he was in his 38th year of living underground. Which if true, may be the modern American record.

I considered blowing Tim off. Better I should find out who was putting mines in my path before walking on them? But as I continued to not see anybody pressing their eyeballs to my windshield, I realized I had a more immediate and compelling need than speculating about the wrath of old Weathermen. I needed a drink.

So at the appointed hour—and for an hour before it, due to my premature ejection from Liz Caruso's condo—I sat on a bar stool at the Casablanca Bar, sipping Scotch and watching college basketball, another of my favorite situations. A guy in a red bandana tapped me on the shoulder. "Mulligatawny," he said.

"Tupac Shakur," I answered.

It turns out he was a pleasant guy.

He was technically underground, but no one was looking for him as far as he knew, and he poked his head above ground from time to time to smell the roses. Like he accepted an allowance from his father, who still loved him and/or had money to burn. And he was shopping for a publisher for his memoirs. "If somebody died because of you, then for the rest of your life somebody's gonna want you caught. But if you just smashed a few storefront windows, who really gives a shit?"

Maybe.

He said he didn't know me from the old days. "Did you change your name?" he asked.

"I was a reporter during the Days of Rage. I wrote a long account of the battle, for my college newspaper...It was reprinted in the..."

"You got gassed?"

"Sure."

"Clubbed?"

"I was wearing a suit and tie."

"Good disguise..."

"It kept me safe. Even though I had long hair..."

"How long?"

"Early Beatles. Tom Hayden. Like that."

"That's not so long. Not Weatherman long. We let it grow out like bikers."

He ordered a Sam Light.

"Who's playing in the game," he asked, pointing to the college basketball on the screen.

"I don't know."

"You're a professor?"

"Assistant Professor."

"Are you well-known?"

"Some people know me."

"Would you write a blurb for my memoirs?"

"You have a publisher?"

"I have to line up my blurbs first..."

"Oh...Well, maybe..." I held up my Scotch to toast his memoirs. He gave my glass a clink.

"Hey," I said, "in the course of your Weather experience did you happen to cross paths with a woman named Samantha Victor?"

"Is that her real name?"

"That's the name she started with. She may have picked up an alias or two..."

"Weather Underground?"

"Yes."

"Days of Rage?"

"Yes."

"With you?"

"Near me."

"Townhouse explosion?"

"Close to it."

"With you?"

"Umm..."

"And your interest in her is?"

"I just want to know if you know her."

"I don't think so...."

"Here's an old picture." I pulled from my wallet the worn and wrinkled snapshot I carried of Samantha, from her high school graduation. Tim looked at it for a long moment. A curl came to his lips which I didn't like at all.

"I may have known her."

I took back my picture.

✱

I STILL BELIEVE IN MY HEART THAT SAMANTHA LOVED ME, maybe not forever, and maybe with a roving eye and a light foot, but there was love. We had fun together. We grew up together, and a few times we exchanged and commingled the deepest parts of our souls. I am not exaggerating—and if somebody wants to quibble or disagree, I don't care—to say we were boyfriend and girlfriend with a couple of short and mostly immaterial gaps from September, 1966 when we met until September, 1967 when she went off to Barnard—the women's college part of Columbia before Columbia itself admitted women a couple years later.

We also spent time together in the summer of 1968. She was living in NYC and deep into her politics, and this hairy asshole Joel, but when she came up to visit her parents she invited me to her house and positioned me between her and them to absorb their attacks. I am not so blind as to call these times a continuation of the love. For what it's worth, Samantha's mother, to the end of her life, telephoned me at random times to tell me how much she hated me.

I almost drove Samantha to Chicago for the Democratic National Convention at the end of August 1968. She asked me if I would, and I said I would (and I undertook a series of awkward schedule adjustments, e.g., quitting my job, to make myself available), but her other travel plans came together at the last minute and I wasn't needed.

I saw her from a distance during the Days of Rage, in October 1969. She wore a helmet and wielded a bat, and shouted orders like a platoon commander. I personally saw her smash the windshield of a Cadillac. I tried to close the distance—not to interfere, or rescue her, but to get a closer look. The terrain was treacherous, however. Cops with batons and shields were massed at the intersections, and the

Weathermen were moving fast and erratically, running for daylight. It was cat and mouse, with tear gas clouds hanging in the air, shards of glass everywhere, rocks thrown. Bunches of well-dressed people stood along the sidewalks like it was a parade, and got gassed.

Those were the days.

✻

BY SUNDAY AFTERNOON I HAD A HEALTHIER HANDLE ON THE LIZ CARUSO EPISODE, and the potential threat to my personal safety. Getting stinking drunk at the Casablanca Bar helped. After Tim left— he said he had dinner plans with old friends from the Movement—I held my stool for an indeterminate number of quarters of college basketball, accompanied by applicable servings of nuts and Scotch. No one telephoned Tim during our interview to scare him away from me, which I took as a positive.

I stumbled through the slushy streets of Harvard Square, bringing back a host of memories, until I found my car. The frosty air sobered me up enough to unlock the door, get in, and fall asleep.

Back in Middletown, Connecticut in the morning, I met Hope Durango, my faculty colleague and budding friend/companion, for brunch. She like me was divorced and a parent of two mostly grown children. She had custody, I did not. She was on okay terms with her ex, I was not. She had money and tenure and exercised regularly. Not so much I.

On the plus side, there no expectation of true love.[5] Companionship was the key concept, or at least that was the stated ground rule. We ordered bloodies. "Hope," I said, 'I'm being followed."

Hope's field was psychology, with excursions into sociology and anthropology. She was also excellent with crossword puzzles. Her ex, a slick Manhattan lawyer now remarried to his young and alluring former secretary, continued to call her for difficult clues. I got the

---

5 Hope: do I mis-describe us?

impression that he was the true love of Hope's life, notwithstanding what a shit he was.[6]

She gave me her usual *Linc-you're-so-nuts-but-I-like-you-anyway* smile, and asked for the facts about why I thought I was being followed. I recounted them, up to and including my concerns with respect to the pointed poker in Liz Seaver Caruso's hands.

"Linc dear, you missed the obvious."

"What do you mean?"

"Liz didn't get a call from a person who was following you..."

"...But..."

"...She got a call back from someone whom she had called earlier to get some background on you. The call back happened to come when you were already there..."

"...No..."

"...Yes..."

"...Hmm..."

"...Liz instigated the call. No one's tracking you."

"...Hmm..."

"Someone may hate you, and think you're a rat, and called her back to tell her that, but he's not out to get you."

"...Hmm..."

I telephoned Liz Caruso that evening. A man answered. 'Hello?"

"Hello, may I speak with Attorney Caruso?"

"Who's calling?"

"Uh, this is a cli...this is Lincoln Cox speaking..."

"Does she know you, Mr. Cox?"

"Yes."

"Hold on please."

He screamed, "Liz."

She screamed back, "What?"

"Telephone."

"Who is it."

---

6 Leonard: nothing personal.

"Lincoln Cox."

"Tell him to fuck himself."

"Liz, pick up the fucking phone and tell him whatever the fuck you want to tell him yourself."

There was muffled shouting, followed by a bang, followed by a dial tone. What a bitch. I called back. She answered this time.

"Hello?" she said.

"Hello, Liz it's..."

"Do you want me to get a court order?"

"No, I..."

"Then stop harassing me."

"I...am sorry. I'm very sorry..."

"...Good..."

"...but I'm not a rat..."

"...That's not what I hear..."

"...Who says? Let me know so I can straighten it out. I don't want to be known as a rat. It's a terrible thing to be known as a rat. Who says I'm a rat?"

"...That's none of your business...."

"...Please..."

"...and don't call me again."

✴

BEFORE MY NEXT CLASS I SIGNALED LIZ'S NIECE LOUISA TO APPROACH MY LECTERN. "I met with your aunt," I said.

"Oh."

"She's very nice."

"Yes."

"Has she told you that we met?"

"Not yet."

"Well, please tell her I thought she was very nice when you speak to her."

"Okay. Did she show you her helmet?"

"No, we didn't get that far."

I've found that nothing good ever comes from getting personal with one's students. Rule #1 is that an old fart is a fool in the arms (in the vicinity) of a young girl, no matter how extenuating and tempting the circumstances, no matter how slight and metaphysical the penetration. Rule #2, which is a corollary of Rule #1, is stick to your own kind. Rule #3, which is a variation of Rule #2, is that if you want a friend, buy yourself a drink.

As Louisa returned to her seat I considered the worst that could happen. Aunt Liz spreads innuendo to Louisa, Louisa spreads to class, someone in class feels duty bound to spread to campus newspaper, which prints it and a hundred students demonstrate outside my condo until the administration rolls over and fires me. I've seen it happen.

Which brings Rule #4 into play, which provides that you can always make matters worse. For example, by way of preemptive action I could ask Louisa to meet me for coffee, to try to sow the seeds of trust, which would likely lead to distrust, and a good chance of disaster.

Whatever. I took a deep breath and moved on to the next chapter, an evaluation of Henry Kissinger's world view, or as I teach it, how he did not win peace for four more years while the lives of an additional 25,000 American soldiers were needlessly sacrificed. "Class," I began non-judgmentally, "in a democracy at war, how much truth should leaders share with the people?"

After class, in the gathered darkness of February at 6:00PM, I headed to the Faculty Club to meet Hope Durango. *En route*, and following serious internal deliberations over whether it's better to act early and needlessly or late and disastrously, I dialed my emergency number.

On the third ring my call was taken. "Answering Service," a female voice said.

"Yes. This is R-251. R-251."

"Thank you for calling, R-251," she said, and disconnected.

I assume, my friend, that you can figure out where I've been and where this is going. You and I aren't children. We're not daydreamers. We know the world isn't black and white. I'm not as clean as I purport to be, or as I wish I were. How about you? Are you lily white and squeaky clean all the way through? I doubt it.

I got a visit after my big article on the Days of Rage in October 1969, my big article that described my run through the streets of downtown Chicago with the Weathermen that was picked up by the national press. I was one of a handful of journalists on the Weatherman side of the police line.

There are historical precedents. I'm thinking for example of the people of Paris in the first flush of the revolution, who ripped down all the religious icons from the walls and stages of Notre Dame Cathedral and replaced them with live dancing by naked women to celebrate the pagan rite of spring. To hell with the rotten fruit of civilization! Or any mass protest after an election is stolen when it seems like all the old bad stuff can be whisked away by concentrated positive thinking. You may recall the attempt to levitate the Pentagon in 1968. See Norman Mailer's account in *Armies of the Night*. Some people said the bricks moved.

The Days of Rage in Chicago in October 1969 was another case of street theater. We—they—were actors with choreographed roles to play on the set—the street—and a moral lesson to deliver to our—their—audience.

The Weathermen's slogan for the Days of Rage was, "Bring the War Home." Let Americans taste the blood and bedlam being perpetrated in Vietnam in the name of America. Let Americans see the light, and rise up against their cynical, manipulative, power-obsessed, money-hungry warlords. America, we are screaming as loud as we can to wake you up before it is too late!

This is the whirlwind you reap when you raise a healthy, well-fed, unscared generation, teach them humane values and secular ideals, convince them that all persons are created equal, and that a person can and should stand up against lies and iniquity, and especially against fascism, and then pull the rug out from under them by imposing a reality which is the antithesis of what they were taught, a reality poised to cause them to die an early and pointless death face down in a rice paddy thousands of miles from home. Some kids will not play by the new rules. Some kids will resist and act out. And I'm not saying I love the Weathermen. I'm just trying to explain what happened.

As I say, I got a visit. From two fellows whose cover story was that they were literary agents—literary agents with short hair, who wore cheap suits, skinny ties, and thick black shoes. I was 21 years old and still God-fearing. They scared the shit out of me.

They walked me to a quiet room in a nondescript building near my dorm. They closed the door and drew the blinds. We all lit up. I smoked Camels, Camels unfiltered. There were no Camels filtered. The literary agents smoked Pall Malls. In those days, those long ago days, everybody smoked cigarettes, and everybody had his own brand. There was a lot of bonding between a man and his brand.

The taller one was Phil. The shorter one was Joe. Phil broke the ice. "Mr. Cox...," he said.

"Please call me Linc. Mr. Cox was my father..."

"Mr. Cox," he continued, "we're not literary agents. We're FBI." He showed me his badge. Joe showed me his badge.

I looked at their badges. I nodded. We all three exhaled a billow of smoke.

"You're in trouble," Phil said.

"What do you mean?"

"We read your Weatherman article. We looked into your history. We think you're a Weatherman."

"No I'm..."

"We think that if you look like a duck, and run through the streets of Chicago like a duck, and smash store windows on Michigan Avenue like a duck, then you're a duck."

"I didn't smash any store windows. I was a reporter. I was reporting."

"We think you're a Weatherman."

"No..."

"Do you approve of people smashing store windows with baseball bats?"

"I don't, but I..."

"You're running with these guys, writing how great they are...what'd you say..." He pulled my article from his breast pocket, unfurled it, and read circled phrases: "...kids with sticks standing up to the mighty military regime...Kids like you and me with the courage to put their bodies and their futures on the line..."

"So what?"

"So what? You're fucking in bed with them that's what..."

"That's not so at all..."

"You're fomenting illegal conduct, to wit a riot..."

"I am not. I'm reporting on what I saw..."

"Are you aware that it's a federal crime to cross state lines with intent to incite a riot?"

"No, I..."

"...or with intent to promote, encourage, participate in or carry on a riot?"

"...No..."

"...or to aid or abet any person in inciting or participating in a riot...?"

"...You are way out of context. I am not..."

"...1968 Civil Rights Act, 18 United States Code, § 210142...Imprisonment for not more than five years, for each violation...The same law they're using against the Chicago Seven applies to you, Linc..."

"Hey, I was a reporter, not a Weatherman. I did not promote rioting for Christ's sake. I did not smash any windows. I stayed on the sidewalk. I was wearing a suit...."

"We have pictures of you with a baseball bat."

"No you don't."

"Yes we do."

"No you don't."

"You support them, don't you?"

"What do you mean?"

"You know what we mean."

"I don't know..."

"Mr. Cox, we mean that you like them. You admire them. You think their cause is just. You want other kids to rally to their cause...Isn't that correct?"

"Well, I..."

So far it was Phil doing the talking. But now Joe started in. "Linc," he said, like I was his nephew, "I know you come from a good family. I spoke to your mother myself, this morning..."

"What?"

"...and I know you're a good student, with a good future ahead of you. I feel very bad about this..."

I don't know exactly which chord Joe plucked, probably his call to my mother. I could feel tears welling up.

"...This hurts your mother, Linc."

"...Yes," I said.

"...She put a lot of her eggs in your basket..."

"Yes," I said.

Obviously as I replay the scene, which I've done quite a few times over the years, I wish I was tougher. I wish I was better prepared, and that I knew I could demand to speak to a lawyer, and that I didn't have to sit there by myself getting grilled like a fucking hamburger. But I was young, not tough, not prepared, and scared as shit.

"This is really too bad," Joe said. "I hate to see your life get ruined."

"Please believe me, I didn't have a baseball bat..."

"It hurts your mother too."

"...and I didn't smash windows. I think it was wrong for them to smash windows. I think they're all crazy..."

"Maybe the judge will give you a break on the sentence...," Phil said.

"...I think..."

"God knows the prisons are crowded enough already..."

"...But..."

I didn't have much fight left. If I were a fish, this is when they would have dropped down the net to scoop me up and bring me into the boat.

"Wait a minute, Phil," said Joe, "there must be something we can do. This is really rough on a nice kid...."

"Yes," I said, "I'm really a nice kid. There must be something..."

Phil shook his head back and forth like there was nothing in the world that he could do. Nothing.

"Please," I said.

"Well," Phil said to me after a long pause, "would you be willing to help us?"

✹

HOPE WAS LATE. So I settled into a comfortable chair at the Club with my Scotch, and watched the evening news on FOX, which happened to include a bit about William (Bill) Ayers, a former Weatherman leader and a favorite target of FOX.

Ayers was on my list of prospective interviewees. He's the son of a wealthy, well-connected, public-spirited Chicagoan. He lived a privileged childhood. He was a 1968 graduate of the University of Michigan, and the former boyfriend of Dianna Oughton (Bryn Mawr, '63). Diana died along with two other Weathermen in the infamous March 6, 1970 explosion of a Greenwich Village townhouse at 18 West 11th Street. Some say the Weathermen were making bombs in the basement of the townhouse for placement and detonation at a non-commissioned officers dance at Fort Dix, New Jersey, with intent to kill and maim. Others say that property not people was the only intended target of Weathermen bombs. It depends on whom you ask, and when you ask them. I wanted to ask Ayers. I had my own understanding.

The townhouse was owned by the father of Cathy Wilkerson (Swarthmore, '66), a Weatherman who narrowly escaped the explosion with her life along with Weatherman Kathy Boudin (Bryn Mawr, '66), daughter of a prominent left-defending NYC attorney, and ironically (some would say) sister of an eminent Federal judge. Eleven years later, on the morning of October 20, 1981, Boudin dropped off her baby son Chesa (Yale '03, Rhodes Scholar, San Francisco DA) with child care, and later that day was in the front seat of a U-Haul truck next to her partner David Gilbert (Columbia, '66, father of Chesa) when it was stopped by two police officers on an exit ramp on the New York Thruway in Nyack, NY, on suspicion of involvement with an armored truck robbery earlier that day at the nearby Nanuet Mall in Nanuet, NY, where $1,600,000 was stolen from a Brinks armored car, and one guard was shot to death. Armed members of the Black Liberation Army who had stolen the money and shot the guard were in the back of the U-Haul when it was stopped on the ramp. They emerged with guns blazing, killing the two police officers.

Boudin was arrested and plea bargained a sentence of 20 years to life for her involvement (as I understand it, under the felony/murder doctrine if a murder is committed in the course of a felony, such as if a police officer gets shot while you're driving a getaway van in the course of fleeing from an armored truck robbery, you can be charged with the murder even if you were just the driver and not the shooter), and was paroled on August 20, 2003. Gilbert was arrested, convicted on three counts of felony manslaughter, and sentenced to 75 years in prison, which when last I checked he is still serving. The disparity between Gilbert's and Boudin's sentences suggests that he and/or the prosecutor viewed his facts and circumstances differently.

Ayers and his wife Bernardine Dohrn (U Chicago, BA '62, JD '67), who like Ayers was a Weatherman leader and organizer of the Days of Rage (October 1969), went underground after the town-house explosion, with charges pending against them from the Days of Rage. But unlike Boudin and Gilbert, who stayed underground, Ayers and Dohrn turned themselves in to authorities in 1980. The charges pending against them were dropped on the grounds of prosecutorial misconduct—illegal searches and wire taps by the FBI in connection with the FBI's extensive and covert Counter Intelligence Program, acronym: COINTELPRO, which sought to infiltrate, disrupt, discredit, and neutralize the activities of a broad range of suspected subversives, including the Weathermen, and whose payroll I was on.

Ayers and Dohrn became the legal guardians of Chesa Boudin (while Chesa's parents did their time). They've lived in Chicago since, where they are said to have been early supporters of Barack Obama's political career.[7]

R-251?

My name was never publicly released as a collaborator. My handlers lived up to that end of the bargain. Which I appreciated and needed, because there's a bad odor attached to being a rat which doesn't wash away. There's also potential for harm, up to and including life-ending harm, if someone is aggrieved by your duplicity and feels duty-bound to not let you get away with it.

Many Weathermen were inherently non-violent, often easy-going and fun-loving—good American kids on the road to becoming rich yuppies, with a healthy upper middle class appreciation for liberal politics, team sports, and brand name products—except the senseless war diverted them into taking a left turn and flirting with violence. When the war ended many of them gathered their wits and retraced their steps back to the mainstream, and may be your doctor or lawyer today, or sit next to you at the symphony or the blackjack table. I wasn't scared of these guys. I was, however, aware of a few who were whack jobs. The Weathermen didn't conduct psychological tests to determine fitness for admission.

There always seemed to be some guy standing around the fringe of a Weatherman

meeting who would erupt at the mention of FBI infiltration, and pledge death to traitors with bone-chilling earnestness. A lot of times these loud guys were the FBI infiltrators. But sometimes not.

My teammates in the FBI have never been excessively concerned for my safety from Weatherman revenge, but have always been

---

7 I don't know any of these famous Weathermen personally. I researched the public record to gather information about them, to prepare for my class.

gravely concerned about my will and ability to expose FBI malfeasance. I don't want to get too far ahead of myself, but R-251 is part of my severance package.

Hope arrived to my corner of the club. She was eager to fill me in on the events of her day. She winked to Walter our waiter, who was my friend too, but liked Hope better. He gave her a return nod, and within seconds was at our little table with a round glass of red wine for madam, and Scottish reinforcement for myself. Which is why I really like going to my club, even if it isn't an especially snooty or exclusive club. I developed (earned) this clubby affection/affectation during my years of exile in jolly England, which was another part of my severance package.

Hope poured forth about... I don't remember what she talked about. It entered one ear, I reacted to it with a smile, grimace, raised eyebrow, head shake, and whatever else I could do to simulate paying attention, and then it departed out the other. Win, win. She was lively and bubbly. I was in my comfortable place. Until my phone buzzed.

"Hello," I said, rising quickly and giving Hope the index finger sign that I apologized for interrupting her story and I'd be back in a minute to hear the rest, but I had to just take this call. I walked at a businesslike pace around intervening tables, chairs and club-goers to and through the door to the back veranda which on summer evenings overlooked the 18th green, as a last straggling golfer putted out in the scented gloaming, and creaked as old crocks rocked their rockers over its slats, and sipped their whiskeys while offering wry commentary on the golfer's approach to his putt and other events of the day, but tonight in the depth of winter was dark, empty and cold.

"This is Maria." She would be the officer on duty.

"Maria, this is R-251."

"What is your PIN number?"

"5022LY."

"Thank you. How may I help?"

"I need support."

"How much?"

"Three," which is to say that my situation was a three on a scale of one to five. I wasn't panicking, just concerned.

"Thank you. Where are you?"

"The usual," which is to say that I'll be at home, and my home address hasn't changed.

"We'll follow up."

"Thank you."

Disconnect. That's your tax dollars hard at work.

At first I didn't think I had sold my soul. I agreed to cooperate a little bit. No big deal. It might be interesting. I'd make a couple bucks, make some contacts, work my own hours, pick my own times to cooperate. As a fringe benefit—in the back of my mind—maybe I could keep closer tabs on Samantha. Maybe, in a perfect world, save her.

Except my new employer viewed it differently.

Phil and Joe set me up with Mike, which wasn't his real name he said at our first meeting in a small chamber deep in the bowels of an ancient basement adjacent to the Harvard campus, lit by a dim bulb swaying on a chord, furnished with two fold-up chairs and a large mouse trap that looked like an instrument of torture in the shadowy light, a chamber seemingly off the beaten track since indoor plumbing was young.

The walls were coated with green-hued plaster, green like lima beans, pockmarked and crumbly although the good news for anyone breathing the stale air was that the plaster was so old that it pre-dated asbestos. Nearby and above-ground, Harvard social rooms were stately and serene, with high ceilings and big windows.

"You like it?" Mike asked.

"Impressive."

"It's my Cambridge office. I use it as a confessional." Mike didn't explain his jokes. I assumed he was kidding, but maybe not.

"You must have a lot of local business these days," I commented. Without attempting to summarize the whole ferment and explosiveness on college campuses back then—you'd have to take my course for that, and do all the reading—suffice to say those days and now are far apart. There were riots, building takeovers, pervasive drugs, ideas that were incomprehensible to the outside world, and significant FBI intrusion.

Mike leaned forward. "Coxy, as of this moment you are my most important piece of on-campus business. I'm going to teach you the basics of clandestine activity..."

"...You're talking to me like I'm a spy..."

"...The first rule is don't get caught. The second rule is don't put yourself in a situation where you might get caught. The third rule is..."

"Seriously Mike, I don't know what they told you about me, but I'm not a spy..."

"Coxy, I don't want to sugarcoat the situation. But you're on our team. We spy."

"That's not me."

"Coxy, I would never threaten you. You're my teammate. And the boys said you were a nice kid. But sometimes it's difficult for us to reverse direction, you know?

"What..."

"How would you feel if it became known that you worked for us?"

"Why would..."

"Exactly. That's why it's important that you play by our team's rules. For your own good. You don't want somebody seeing your picture in *Ramparts*, with a caption..."

"What?"

"...Let me tell you something, Coxy. I've been tracking Communists for thirty years, in all their subversive disguises. The Weathermen are just the newest version..."

"...Mike, I don't think so. They're college kids..."

"...Coxy, how do you think all the campus unrest got started?"

"...The War in Vietnam..."

"...Not so, my naïve young friend. The Communists started it. They'd like you to think that students across America woke up one morning and started marching and protesting and taking over buildings because of the War. But the fact is the Communists were laying kindling and stoking the flame for years. They sent their best agitators from campus to campus, Columbia to Berkeley and all points in between. These guys were trained to recruit disaffected kids, and turn them into Commies. They knew how to use bull horns and mimeograph machines. They were geniuses at provoking college administrators to overreact. They, my naïve young friend, started it."

"Mike, you're making this stuff up."

"I wish."

Mike was my first handler. I guess one always has affection for one's first handler. But not so much me for Mike. We came to a parting of the ways. I heard he died recently. I didn't send condolences.

I had weekly sessions with Mike in his subterranean confessional during November and the beginning of December 1969. The sessions lasted fifty minutes. They ended with Mike handing me cash and warning me not to fuck up.

He spent a lot of time on how to get to and from sessions without being remembered. His mantra was that it's not the end of the world to be observed, as long as you aren't remembered. He spent time on leaving messages, making calls, operating a tape recorder, picking a lock, hiding in a trash bin, following a suspect by car and on foot, basically an introductory course on spy craft, with sidetracks into the history of the American Communist Party.

Mike gave me my first official assignment on the eve of the holidays. "Coxy, what're you doing for Christmas?"

"Not much."

"There's a Weatherman meeting next Wednesday the 23rd, at Columbia."

"Open to the public?"

"Not exactly. But I think it may be open to friendly fellow travelers. Such as yourself."

"How did I find out about it?"

"You're the press. You have sources."

So I went. I took the shuttle on Tuesday afternoon, compliments of Uncle Sam, although in those days the shuttle was ridiculously cheap for students, and you could smoke on the plane, and didn't have to have your shoes inspected because nobody was crazy enough to blow up a plane they were flying in.

I stayed the night at my friend's mother's apartment on the East Side, which is something I might have done anyway as a destination for my holiday, in case anyone was asking. I took a cab to Columbia on Wednesday morning, and walked around the campus intending not to be remembered. It was my first time there. Coming from Harvard, I wasn't impressed.

The air was cold and smelled of what I thought was toasted nuts but which since then has been explained to me as the aroma of grime and fumes. With a hint of something excremental blowing in from the river. The clouds were thick and low. Snow was predicted. I could have used a heavier sweater beneath my parka, and a pair of gloves. I carried a dark green faux-canvas bag with a black strap. It held my paper and pens, and a portable tape recorder which was as bulky as a toaster, and some reading material including the John Milton text-book that I lugged everywhere and never opened until the eve of the exam when I realized it was hopeless and opted for Cliff Notes. Thank God for Cliff Notes. In a sensible world you would read Cliff Notes before taking the course. If you got anything more from the lectures it would be gravy. Even at Harvard.

The Weatherman meeting was scheduled for noon in a tiered classroom on the first floor of a big old building that fronted on a quad (I have no idea whether the meeting was approved or even known about by university authorities). With the students on vacation the quad was quiet. I walked past the front door of the meeting building at 11:45AM on a scouting mission, and returned at 11:55AM for an attempted entry.

A bulky fellow with a ponytail filled space on the warm side of the door. As I stepped inside, he said, "Hey, I've been watching you."

So much for blending into the landscape, so as not to be remembered. I was a work in progress.

"Why were you watching me?" I asked.

"What are you doing here?" he asked back.

"Why do you care?"

"Who are you?"

"Who are you?"

"I asked first."

"I don't give a shit."

Sort of a stand-off. Apparently the building also had back doors, side doors and trap doors—may have been chosen for its plenitude of ingresses and egresses, in case of fire, or FBI emergency—because scruffy Weather-looking folks were emerging from the woodwork and congregating near the bulky fellow and me, greeting each other with hearty Weather hugs.

"Why don't you hassle those guys?" I asked him.

"I know them."

"Who are they?"

"Who are you?"

Which is when Samantha Victor walked by, not easily recognizable as a former chiffon-clad deb. She wore heavy boots, jeans, a surplus army jacket, and a red bandana. She wasn't advertising her beauty. I'm not saying I heard violins, under these gritty circumstances, but even her downscale look managed to tighten my air intake and wobble my knees.

"Samantha," I said.

She stopped short and did a double take. "Holy shit," she said. "Lincoln Cox what the fuck are you doing here?" She gave me a big hug, like I was family, maybe an older brother. Pardon me for burying my nose into the side of her neck, and refueling.

"You are a sight for sore eyes," she said, pushing me back and holding me at bay.

"I'm reporting. I heard there's a meeting here."

"Ah. That's right. You're a famous reporter. I read your Days of Rage story. Very impressive..."

"Thank you."

"But you came down a little harsh on the Weathermen."

"Some people say I wrote it like I was a Weatherman."

"Who? The FBI?"

She smiled, confirming that she was being funny. I smiled back.

"Samantha," I said in a low voice, for her ears only, "you know I will always..."

She put her hand to my mouth. "Linc, shhh. Don't say it."

✳

DO I HAVE A CLUE AS TO WHY SAMANTHA BECAME A WEATHERMAN? The quick answer is that she met this creepy guy named Joel at the beginning of her freshman year at Barnard (Fall, 1967). He was a big campus radical, and all his friends were big campus radicals. They sat around and drank wine and plotted to take over the university. By November she was one of them. But that doesn't explain why she picked him when—in my opinion at least—she could have picked anyone.

Joel was a firebrand, rousing with a crowd, lean and long-haired, a bad boy in the Che Guevara mold. I saw him in action. I thought he was a complete phony. Which was sort of proven out by the fact that by the time of the Days of Rage, when Samantha was smashing car windows with her baseball bat, old Joel was retired from the Movement and going to law school.

I know Samantha was angry at her mother for being such an hysteric, and fumbling her life away. And her father was a concrete block if ever I've seen one, incapable of emotional expression except for rage and intolerance, like the time he tried to kill me with Samantha's baseball bat because he thought (erroneously) that I was the lucky guy in her life. But that parental combo has probably also produced well-adjusted brain surgeons and acrobats.

Which is to say that the older I get the more willing I am to accept a random walk explanation for a lot of curious personality outcomes. Samantha, in her flower-strewn, marijuana-welcoming openness as a freshman, could as well have been swept away by a wavy-haired teaching assistant in English 101, and become a fervent poet's muse. Nothing ineluctable about it. Luck of the draw.

A more apt question for me arises as to why I, having been royally rebuffed by her in my romantic overtures since 1967—pre-Joel—persisted, kept her on a pedestal, thought she was the only one, saw hope when there was none, and would have caught a bullet on her behalf if given the opportunity. What peculiar life circumstances laid this trap for me?

"This is a closed meeting," Samantha told me. "Members only."

"But Samantha…Can you get me in?"

"Wait here a second."

She circulated among the milling crowd, pleading my case I hoped and assumed with those who made admission decisions, hugging and being hugged by some scraggly beasts, and returned to me with a room pass. "But listen," she said, "just sit quietly in the back, and don't embarrass me. I vouched for you."

"No problem."

I knew Mike would be pleased if I recorded the meeting. When people finished hugging and settled into their seats, with me by myself in the back row, crouched and sleepy-eyed so as to minimize curiosity, I casually reached into my green bag and flicked on the record switch.

They didn't start with the Pledge of Allegiance.

They started instead with a shouting match over who was in charge of the meeting.

Bear in mind (so the story is told by some, and disputed by others) that this was after the split with Progressive Labor (PL), the faction of SDS that drew inspiration from Mao until he dishonored himself by breaking bread with Richard Nixon; the faction that truly believed in the prophesies of Marx, was in the class struggle for the long haul and not just until the War ended, was short-haired and focused (no offense intended), wore short-sleeve collared shirts rather than the hippie attire favored by the more flamboyant Weathermen, was more likely from Brooklyn than a fancy suburb, was happiest when they had a factory to organize, or even better a factory to occupy and defend against the hired thugs of the counter revolutionaries, and was expelled and/or walked out from SDS in the summer of 1969 on ideological grounds reminiscent of the purges and schisms that befell the Bolsheviks, and other true believers before and since.

Go left or get left.

A woman and a man sat in folding chairs on stage, facing the audience. Our leaders.

A jock-type fellow in the front row with a luxurious ponytail stood up, and kicked it off. "Who picked you to sit up there?" he said, pointing at the woman on stage.

"Sit down, Stan," the woman said, "you're making a scene..."

"You sit down..."

"Stan, this isn't about you and me. This is about politics..."

"Darlene, are you fucking that guy?" Stan said, pointing at the guy on stage next to Darlene.

"Stan, you live in a bourgeois bubble. You totally miss the point..."

"Fuck you..."

"Stan, you've changed. Your politics is reactionary. I don't like it..."

The audience was with Darlene. They picked up on her disdain, and hooted Stan, called him a pig, gave him two thumbs down. He glowed red and exasperated. He looked around for support and found none.

Darlene, with the crowd at her feet, fixed Stan with a cold and hard eye. I ducked from it, and I was twenty rows away. She was one tough, don't-fuck-with-me radical woman. "All those in favor of purging Stan raise your hand...," she said.

Most hands were quickly raised, including Samantha's, and mine.

"Stan, you're out of here," Darlene announced, casually like she was tossing the trash.

The next item on the agenda concerned tactical violence. A mousy girl with a shy demeanor walked to the front. She nodded to the leaders, and cleared her throat. She gave Stan a chance to let the door close behind him. She reminded me of studious girls I knew at school, with and without thick glasses, who were easy to overlook.

"Our message is crippled by liberal values," she screamed in high volume from the first syllable, so shrill I feared she might flummox my tape recorder and shatter the light bulbs. I did not expect such a big voice from so meek a stature. I guessed the union made her strong.

"Peaceful protest doesn't work. Smashing windows doesn't work. Liberalism doesn't work. Liberalism is all about talk and concessions, and being polite, and it's DOA...DOA...DOA...," she screamed. People in the seats rose and screamed "DOA" back at her.

"...If we really want to bring the War home, we have to by-pass weak-assed liberalism, and be willing to tolerate consequences! If it's bloodshed...if it's casualties...it's fighting fire with fire. It's the greater good!"

More people stood and cheered. One woman called, "Right on, sister," and others continued to repeat "DOA." But there wasn't universal acclaim. This call to arms wasn't nearly as popular as purging Stan. I saw folks roll their eyes. I saw others staring into space. Darlene, our leader, didn't reveal herself.

Samantha was sitting between two guys, each of whom I thought was more intent on getting her attention than on participating in the public agenda. The one whispered in her left ear. She laughed. The other tried her right ear, and unless I was hallucinating he gave that ear a little nibble. Another laugh from her. I thought I was poolside in the Bahamas.

✸

HOPE DURANGO ACCOMPANIED ME HOME FROM THE CLUB, as she sometimes did, we being grown-ups and unencumbered, and friends, and compatible. I—and I think I speak for her on this point[8]— was not looking for the ensnarement of a deeper intimacy.

My wish was to skim the emotional surface. Her ex-husband's name was Leonard. He was a shit to her, as she often recited, but she

---

8 Yes?

unaccountably still loved him. Fine, no problem for me.

"Who called you at the club?" she asked me.

"That was just an old piece of business."

"You have secrets, Linc."

"No, I'm as transparent as..."

"...as what? A brick?"

"...a pane of glass..."

Hope didn't have to know about my tour of duty with the FBI. Jill, whom I was married to for a decade, didn't know. Of course, Jill didn't care. She was busy keeping a lid on her own secrets, and was English and imperviously ignorant of the twists and turns of American politics. Worked undercover for the FBI? Sounds like the patriotic thing to do.

My cell rang at midnight. "Hello."

"Your service call is here."

So was Hope, still. "Who's that" she asked.

"I'll tell you in the morning. Go back to sleep."

Did I mention that Hope had some anthropology in her? She was a good digger, and expert at connecting the fragments. By morning she had put together a pretty good picture.

"Who visited in the middle of the night?" she asked.

"A neighbor lost his cat."

"It reminds me of the time you told me that someone was tracking you down in Boston..."

"...You dispelled that, remember?"

"...I gave you a credible alternative..."

"...It appeased me..."

"...Still I wondered why you were so quick to think someone was tracking you down. Normally you aren't so paranoid..."

"...I try to keep my paranoia chained to the bed..."

"...But now I think someone might actually be tracking you..."

"...Why would someone do that?"

"...Maybe a debt collector..."

"...Oh?"

"...Who do you owe?"

"...American Express. Verizon. Audi Financial. Wells Fargo Bank..."

"...Do you owe the Weathermen?"

✳

THE SHIT HIT THE FAN AT THE TOWNHOUSE AT 18 WEST 11TH STREET—JUST OFF FIFTH AVENUE, in a tony, high-end Greenwich Village neighborhood, in the heart of Manhattan—just before noon on Friday, March 6, 1970. The *Times* reported three explosions and a raging fire. The first blast "...powerful enough to tear a hole in the front wall of the building, apparently occurred in the basement of the townhouse..." NYT, March 7, 1970. The two subsequent blasts were lighter, triggered when the first blast burst the gas lines. Flames engulfed the building.

The totality of destruction made recovery work slow and difficult. It took days of picking through rubble for the authorities to conclude that the recovered body parts constituted the remains of three victims. It took longer still for the authorities to propose a plausible explanation, that the three dead were Weathermen, who were building anti-personnel bombs in the basement—bombs packed with roofing nails and dynamite—and that by accident and/or incompetence their bombs burst prematurely.

It is reported that at least two persons in the building survived the blast—Kathy Boudin and Cathy Wilkerson (Wilkerson's father is said to have owned the townhouse and be on vacation in the Caribbean at the time). I imagine the survivors huddling among the first wave of rescuers, but disappearing in a New York minute before I or anyone else at the scene made sense of things.

The public record is not clear on what the Weathermen wanted to do with their bombs. Some commentators have opined that the plan was to detonate the bombs that night at a dance for noncommissioned officers at Fort Dix, New Jersey. Few commit to whether a warning call to the dance was part of this plan, or would have become part of the plan as the time to detonate drew closer. Some Weathermen argued that it was time to take the gloves off—time to sacrifice people in order to wake them up—but others resolutely opposed this idea. For what it's worth, the Weathermen did explode bombs before and after March 6, 1970, all of which (as far as I know) were aimed at property, all of which (as far as I know) were aimed at property, followed warning calls, and killed no one.[9]

Here's what else I know.

Following up on my intelligence gathering, the FBI tracked Stan, the guy who was purged from the pre-Christmas Columbia U. meeting, thinking he might be available to join our team on account of the bad way he was treated by their team. I understand that the FBI was especially pleased for a hook-up with Stan because of his purported intimacy with a Weatherman female leader, which was catnip.

My guys, Phil and Joe, drew the assignment to turn Stan. They were viewed as experts at turning kids, although I wouldn't give them such high marks. They got a lucky bounce with me.

Stan had rich parents, which tends to be part of the Weatherman *pro forma*. His father was a corporate executive. His family lived on Central Park West, with a beautiful view of the park, Mike told me after he had cased the joint and placed the bug. They also had a country house in Connecticut, which is where Stan retreated to after his Weatherman career was abruptly ended, to pass the time until his draft physical. His lottery number was 31, which was like a bull's eye on his back.

Mike and Joe made their move on Stan on a Saturday afternoon, when he was alone in the country house. They had him on tape telling his parents how much he regretted his time with the Weathermen, how the Weathermen were childish, closed-minded, and counter-productive, and how he just wanted to go back to school if he could figure out a way to not get drafted, which got his mother crying that she had her son back.

---

9 Reader, please let me know if you know different.

But he was a tougher nut than they expected. He didn't let them into the house. He didn't give them a chance to roll out their spiel. He kept them chilling on his doorstep while he called his dad for advice, a call that ended abruptly when his savvy dad said he didn't trust the privacy of their line. Stan came back to the door and told Phil and Joe to pound sand.

Stan was so pissed at the FBI's heavy tactics that he decided he had to warn the Weathermen about what the FBI was doing, even though he'd sworn he'd never have anything to do with the Weathermen again. Which is how the FBI got to the Wilkerson townhouse on West 11th Street. Stan led them to it.

When Stan drove to the townhouse in lieu of the risk of telephoning his warning, the FBI was with him like head lice on a hippie. High fives all around. I got a commendation. And the plot thickened.

On the afternoon of Wednesday, March 4, 1970, I was leaning against a third-floor picture window overlooking West 11th Street, as close to the Wilkerson townhouse as we could discretely get. With me in the room, sitting around a card table or splayed on the big couch or playing with electronic gear on the floor was our stake-out team, our team leader Bill Flynn, his supervisor Barry Flynn (no relation) up from Washington D.C., and four agents specializing in bugs, bombs, break-ins, and all-around surveillance and crime prevention. Everybody smoked. The ashtrays overflowed.

Inside the townhouse the Weathermen came and went, dropping off groceries and dynamite (we thought). We had their phone bugged, and kept a photo log of arrivals and departures, and made one bold, quick and risky inspection of the interior of the townhouse under the guise of checking the gas meter in the basement. I was on the team as an alternate, available if my play was called, but probably just there for pizza. They called me "kid."

Our game plan was in a dilemma. To swoop in and arrest now, on charges of possessing dynamite (we thought) without a permit, conspiracy to do indeterminate bad things, occasionally smoking dope and acting un-American, with the expected outcries from a battalion of lefty lawyers about illegal wiretapping, and their hand-wringing motions urging the judge to throw out the evidence and let the kids walk, argued in favor of patience. To be patient and wait until the kids blew up the Empire State Building, argued in favor of a preemptive strike. Bill Flynn urged patience. Barry Flynn asked for preemption proposals.

We had the townhouse's building plans and the street's infrastructure plans spread across the table. "I think," Frank C said, "we can access the exterior wall of the basement from the street...via the utility channel..." Frank was our break-in genius. "We can pick through the wall and set up a camera...Or move around a few old bricks and crawl inside. I've seen a lot harder..."

"I think we should do another check of the gas meter," said Dana, who played the role of gas inspector the first time around. "I sold it. There were no suspicions. Nobody, not even a Commie, wants a gas leak..."

"You know where I stand on this," said Murray, who had been advocating a frontal assault all along, along the lines of the Fred Hampton bust in Chicago the prior December, when Hampton, the charismatic twenty-one-year-old Black Panther leader who was reputed to be a major aggravant to J. Edgar Hoover and Hoover's vision of American propriety, was shot dead in his bed, purportedly resisting arrest. The jury was still out on that as a role model for proper law enforcement. Some called it murder.

"Murray," Barry Flynn said, "you may have the best solution, quick, straightforward, let the chips fall as they may...You have a cancer, you cut it out..." Barry inhaled deeply on his Lucky Strike, a brand which I thought smoked too dry, unlike my rich, throat-soothing Camels. "There is support at high levels for your viewpoint...but..." Barry exhaled, letting his plume finish his sentence for him.

"...There's always a 'but,'" Murray said, underlining his disappointment with a big plume of his own.

"...Murray, listen," Barry continued, "we are just too much in the dark here. The political and public relations consequences of getting caught with our pants down are enormous. And we can't count on the press to understand the situation, like they used to. They smoke as much marijuana as the hippies. And when they think of the Weathermen they don't think Commie scum, they think 'Stop the War in Vietnam'…We need to know more before we act…"

"That's a relief," Bill Flynn chimed in. "I was afraid we were about to preemptively blow the place up…Hah, hah…"

Barry Flynn gave a sideways glance to Bill Flynn, and blew some more smoke. "My call," Barry said, "is to run with the kid."

"Huh?" we all answered.

"Kid," he said to me, "I want you to ring their bell, flash the peace sign, and ask to be let in for an interview…"

"What if they ask me how I happened to pick their bell from all the other bells in New York City?"

"…You don't have to give up your sources. You're the press…"

"…Yes, but…"

"…and I think they'll welcome someone who'll tell their side of the story…"

"…Maybe, but…"

"…and if we're lucky you'll get a visual of their dynamite…"

"…I…I…"

"…and the downside risk is limited. They're not the Mafia. They won't kill you if they find out you're a rat…I don't think…"

So I rang their bell. At 10:00AM on Thursday, March 5, 1970, in broad daylight, more curious than fearful, not thinking about whether I was good or bad, or righteous or treacherous, just focused on accomplishing my mission. I found the courage of a good soldier.

A female Weatherman answered the bell. She opened the door a few inches, enough so I could see her face. "Yes," she said to me, slightly irritable as she might have been if I were selling vacuum cleaners door to door, and she was interrupted in the middle of her favorite soap.

"I'm Lincoln Cox, a reporter for my student newspaper. I've written articles about the Weathermen, which you may have read, favorable articles…"

"So?"

"I'm told that there are Weathermen staying here…"

"I don't know what you're talking about."

"Please, I'm not the cops. I'm anti-war. My paper is anti-war. I just want to talk…" I gazed around at the street—like I was scanning windows for snipers, like I was feeling exposed standing there on the doorstep in plain view—in an effort to demonstrate my solidarity with my generation's universal fear of being suddenly busted.

She paused for a moment in her show of irritation and disinterest, which felt to me like a nibble. It dawned on me that I had to give her more line. She would have to consult with others, and wouldn't want to do that while I chilled on her steps drawing attention of neighbors and street traffic. I said, "I'm going. I'll come back in a few minutes."

The door closed behind me. But she didn't slam it. She didn't say, "Don't bother, creep," which I took note of, and construed as a positive. I headed east to Fifth Avenue, at a businesslike pace, assuming I was followed by the stake-out boys, and possibly by a Weatherman or two, who in turn were followed by more stake-out boys. I kept moving for twenty minutes, pausing at a store window here and there to emulate a casual pedestrian and/or to let everybody catch up, and ending at the point of beginning. I re-rang the bell.

This time the door opened, and I was invited in.

✺

AFTER HOPE DURANGO FIGURED OUT THAT I HAD UNFINISHED HISTORY WITH THE WEATHERMEN, she sniffed like a bloodhound for more details. "Were you recruited by the FBI? Did they pay you? Are you still being paid?"

At first I was coy and buttoned-up with my answers, but Hope kept sniffing, and kept re-filling my glass with Johnny Walker Black until—besotted, outwitted, and tired of keeping ancient secrets—I dropped my guard and let her have her way with me. "Yes, they paid me."

"Do you feel badly about that now?"

"Yes, I do. I was weak..."

"You were young..."

"I was dishonorable."

"Linc, everyone does things when they're young that they regret afterwards. The Weathermen look back at what they did with regret..."

"Some of them..."

"Besides, who says that what you did was dishonorable? What loyalty did you owe to the Weathermen?"

"Not so much to the Weathermen as to..." I trailed off, thinking of Samantha Victor.

Hope was gentle, yet relentless. She sucked out all my secrets, except for a few about Samantha and a few others about the concluding events of March 6, 1970, which were well-hidden in the sub-basement of my brain, and not accessible without a warrant and a crowbar.

"Hope," I asked her in the darkness of my bedroom, as I lay drained and relieved to have unloaded upon her, as our two hearts beat almost as one, or closer to one and a quarter since mine was still racing, "are you interested in the Weathermen?"

"Yes."

"You know my book project about them? I'm doing an exposition of where are they now?"

"Yes."

"Would you like to work with me on my book project?"

"Are you proposing?"

"Yes."

"I do."

The next Saturday morning we undertook our first joint assignment. We took an early train to Manhattan for a noon meeting at the Starbucks on Broadway and West 81st with Eric Feather[10], an

---

10 This is another replacement name. I don't know why I latched onto it. Maybe because a

ex-Weatherman who went on to become a psychiatrist with an A-list Upper West Side clientele. He was there when we arrived, sipping a *grande* in a corner sitting spot, his long legs stretched out, his silver hair slicked back, recognizable from his photograph on the back flap of his recent best-selling book about deprogramming cult kids, and getting them into a good college, though the photograph didn't do justice to his honker of a nose. In the flesh it was an eye-catcher, bulbous and so shiny you could even say it glowed. No doubt it must have turned some of his talking patients cross-eyed.

But outside of his nose, Dr. Feather was a put together man, a put together New York City man by which I mean—in my experience as an observer of these things—physical oddities don't detract in New York City, they're often esteemed, as long as they're backed by money which his nose appeared to be in that he wore an expensive-looking casual shirt under a soft leather zipper jacket, black jeans with a fancy buckle, and boots, sort of a dude cowboy West Side shrink look. I'm going into detail because Dr. Feather was a man to be reckoned with. He was reputed to be the hub in the flow of current Weathermen information. A key interviewee. A big fish. A source of many secrets.

He was absorbed by his coffee and his *Times*. Seemingly oblivious to the Starbucks bustle around him. His eyes, if you could get over his nose, were deep-set and dark, suggesting that he had seen his share of things.

We introduced ourselves to him with a round of hellos and handshakes. He was courtly. I left Hope to chitchat while I went to the bar to get our coffees, bold *grandes* without need for space for milk, double-cupped and sleeved for a cooler hold.

I'd been mulling over the morality of revenge as a talking point with Dr. Feather, when is it too old and cold to be consummated, and when is it not. I considered Nazi hunters, who extend no mercy to their elderly prey, pleased to pull them from wheelchairs in nursing homes without concession to the passage of time. I considered

---

feather blows in the wind.

Michael Corleone, who killed all the enemies of his family—Sollozzo, Captain McLusky, Carlo Rizzi, the Sicilian guy in the Buffalo pizzeria who blew up Michael's first wife in Sicily, and Fredo, Michael's weak and pathetic older brother who posed no threat to Michael at the time he was killed.

I presented my thoughts on the subject to Dr. Feather and Hope when I returned with the coffee. "You realize," Dr. Feather replied, "that each of Michael Corleone's acts of revenge was first degree murder. The American legal code does not take exception for crimes of revenge ..."

"My take," Hope said, "is that Michael's acts of revenge ruined his soul. In the end—I'm referring to I and II not III—..."

"...Of course," Feather and I chimed in.

"...he was a lost and lonely man, with blood, lots of blood, on his hands. I think the moral of the story is that revenge must be tempered with mercy. Michael should have been merciful to Fredo."

I nodded. Michael should have been merciful to Fredo. Fredo posed no threat to Michael. Michael's lack of mercy to Fredo was cold.

"Why so interested in revenge on this bright Saturday?" Feather asked.

"I'm wondering whether in your dealings with various former Weathermen, Weathermen whom you come in contact with, you know, whether you find they are still revengeful after all these years."

"Revengeful? Against whom?"

"Against the FBI, the war people, maybe friends who they think betrayed them, for an example."

"Why do you ask?"

"Oh, you know, from my academic perspective I'm interested in how the passage of time smooths the rough edges, and puts things into perspective..."

"Someone called him a name," Hope blurted out.

"That's not it at all," I said.

"He's bent out of shape because someone called him a name, and he thinks the person wants to kill him or something."

"Not at all," I said. I gave Hope a "shut up" glance.

"What name was he called?" Dr. Feather asked.

"A rat," said Hope.

"No, Hope," I said, "that's incorrect. You're way off track…"

"Who called him that?" Dr. Feather asked. "An old Weatherman?"

"No, no, no," I said. "Hope is all mixed up…"

"Yes, an old Weatherman," Hope said.

"A rat?" said Dr. Feather.

"I'm not a rat," I said.

We all took a sip of coffee. In the old days we probably would have filled our lungs with smoke, and mulled the variables of the moment under the influence of tobacco product chemicals. So I guess if I'm evaluating whether anything good has happened in the last forty years, the reduction of cigarette smoking is one good thing. But I was peeved as hell at Hope and her big mouth. I was not expecting or prepared to share my rat business with Dr. Feather, regardless of how wise or esteemed he might be.

"That's a funny story," Dr. Feather said.

"I'm not a rat."

"Fine," he said. "Let's just assume for purposes of our discussion that you're thinking about revenge in the abstract…" He allowed a crinkly smile to creep around his nose, suggesting that I was amusing to him, like a squeaky toy rat to a cat. "You're thinking if, in the event some old Weatherman were to call you a rat, would that pose a risk of harm to you?"

"No," I said.

"Yes," Hope said.

"I'm sure you realize," Dr. Feather said, "that not all Weathermen had the benefit of sane and balanced personalities. We were an extreme group. We attracted extreme personalities. I'm sure some of them—some of us—were dangerous to ourselves and to others, and should have been culled and committed. And if those ones are still alive today, they're probably still crazy."

"You think?" Hope asked.

"I can't give you much comfort on this," he said. "Crazy people do crazy things."

"Interesting," Hope said.

"Good to know," I said.

"So, when were you called a rat?" Dr. Feather asked.

"It doesn't matter."

"He was in Boston," Hope said, "talking with Elizabeth Seaver..."

"Elizabeth Seaver Caruso?"

"Yes. Do you know her?" Hope asked.

"An old and dear friend, all the way back to the Days of Rage for goodness sake. I ran the streets with her. A fast and agile runner. We stay in touch. She's blossomed nicely..."

"He was sitting in her parlor..." Hope said.

"Okay, Hope. Fine. Enough already."

"Linc, let's just get it out on the table. Maybe Dr. Feather can help you talk it through..."

Dr. Feather smiled. He was a big cheese kind of guy.

"Okay, fine," I said. "I'll tell it. I was sitting with Elizabeth Seaver Caruso in her parlor when she got a call from an ex-Weatherman who somehow knew I was there with her..."

"...Maybe he was returning her call," Dr. Feather said, "and just happened to call while you were there..." Hope nodded. That was her point.

"...And she told me that he told her that I'm a rat, which I'm not..."

Feather's left leg twitched. I thought he was reacting to my remark, like he was raising an eyebrow via his sciatic nerve. But instead he reached down and pulled his buzzing blackberry from his pants pocket. He looked at its face for a second and excused himself to take a call. He exited through the coffee klatches and to the sidewalk in a few long strides, nose first. Hope and I observed him through the window.

"What do you make of him?" Hope asked me.

"I'm annoyed at you for talking so much."

"It was obvious what you were trying to say. I just helped you get there."

"No you didn't."

"I didn't say anything bad."

"My personal stuff is none of his business."

"He's a famous shrink. I thought he might be helpful, at no charge. What bad thing could he do?"

"That's not how I think about it."

"Okay, sorry. How about his schnozz?"

I shook my head, in response to both her mouth and his schnozz. We sipped coffee.

"He's quite a refined man," Hope went on. "It's hard to imagine him running through the streets with a baseball bat…"

I shook my head to that too, and raised an eyebrow as if to say, "I'm not talking to you, but I agree that the idea of a young Feather running through the streets with a baseball bat is a brain-teaser…" Like when you see the grown child of an old friend. Or the old friend himself, curled and dragging a leg. Occasionally the passage of time stares you in the eye, and demands a salute.

Feather walked back in. "Sorry," he said, "my patient thought this would be a good day to go crazy…"

"Oh my," said Hope. "Do you have to go?"

"No," Feather said as he settled back into his seat, "I talked her off the ledge…"

"Oh my," said Hope.

"…metaphorically speaking," Feather said.

"That's a relief," said Hope, who to her credit was quite big-hearted, and trusting. "Do you keep up with a lot of old Weathermen?" I asked.

"I do. I'm a public figure. I'm listed in the phone book. They find me. They talk to me…"

"Albert W?" Hope asked.

"Albert…He's the guy who enlisted after Chicago?"

"Yes, doctor." Hope said. "You know your Weathermen."

"I do."

"He's next on our list of interviewees."

"An interesting fellow."

"How about Samantha Victor?" I asked. "Did you know her?"

"Samantha Victor?"

"Did you know her?"

"Free-spirited," he said, again with the crinkly smile, like it was bittersweet to recall Samantha Victor. "Drove the boys crazy."

"Do you know what happened to her?"

"I do," he said, and paused as though collecting his thoughts or counting his words. I feared he would say that Samantha was dead. I braced for that shock.

"...She's...doing okay," he said.

"...Oh," I said. And being a complete fool, I could hear that old Samantha music rising in my head. "Where is she?"

He gave me a look, like I was trespassing.

"Do you know where she is?" I asked again.

"Why so interested in Samantha Victor?"

"I..."

Feather's crinkly smile turned into a wise-ass grin, akin to a sneer, like now he knew exactly who I was and how I got there. "I get it. You're a member of the Samantha club..."

"No, no. I knew her a long time ago, briefly. It was nothing. I'm not a member...I would like to interview her for my book, that's all."

"Yes," he said, "I see."

His leg twitched again. He glanced at his phone screen. "Excuse me," he said as he walked outside.

"Samantha Victor," Hope said. "Hello? You're holding back about her, aren't you?"

"She was a long time ago. Before there were Weathermen..."

"A girlfriend?"

"Maybe."

"First love?"

"Maybe."

"She left you?"

"I guess that's what happened, although..."

"Although what?"

"Although..." I sat there without words to finish the clause. I looked at the pretty baristas. I smelled the coffee. I did a minute of time travel back to a perfumed evening in September 1966. So shoot me.

Feather re-entered, now appearing hot and bothered, his big nose red as a ripe tomato. Something was up.

"She's back on the ledge?" Hope asked.

"No...but I have a report on you, Mr. Lincoln Cox. You *are* a rat."

"What?"

"You were a traitor to the best people of your generation...You have blood on your hands...I curse you, and wish you no peace..."

Exit Feather, in a huff.

✳

LET'S GO BACK TO THE TOWNHOUSE.

After my walk around the block, I re-rang the front doorbell. This time I was invited in and escorted to the living room. One of those lovely, understated, stylish New York rooms, with oil paintings on the walls. It is a shame on many levels that the place was blown to smithereens.

A semi-circle of Weathermen was there to greet me. Some faces I'd seen before, but grimmer now than I remembered from our Columbia meeting a few months before, and uniformly dressed in Army surplus attire, i.e., the green jackets with lots of pockets, the heavy boots, none of the hippie love beads or psychedelic colors that I was used to seeing on them, and that still adorned the youth of America at large. The Weathermen had moved on. Their times they had a-changed.

Six, sometimes seven of them. Their number varied as they drifted in and out of the room.

It's fair to say that most of America wasn't tuned in or turned on to the Weathermen's cause at that moment in history. With the advent of President Nixon, America was drifting toward law and order, and fear of the counterculture. The counterculture itself was drifting away from politics, and becoming a leisure time activity—hair was long, skirts were short, rock and roll was loud, marijuana was in high school.

The mainstream of the anti-war movement watched the Weathermen from a safe distance, and stayed dedicated to non-violence and related liberal values. It wrung it's hands in the face of the endless war, and proposed more marches, getting very good at the logistics of marches. The press and media were mouthpieces of the Establishment, with few exceptions, and the Nixon administration was making steady progress in minimizing the exceptions, with special attention as I recall to the tax returns of anti-war reporters. No women or minorities in the press. No lefties or youths. Lots of hard-drinking, hidebound members of a fraternity whose reference point was the Cold War, and to whom the Weathermen were a freak show.

Only the FBI, which was dedicated to shutting down left wing subversives and preserving the political *status quo*, was paying close attention to the Weathermen, and taking them seriously, as seriously as the Weathermen thought they deserved to be taken, as seriously as the windmill took Don Quixote. Or maybe the other way around.

I don't mean to preach—and God knows I'm no one to preach—but I think it is nuts that America now welcomes a prosperous trading partnership with Vietnam, but has not connected these dots to the 54,000 Americans who died there just a few years ago, with the obvious conclusion that these boys died in vain, that they were led over a cliff by leaders who deserve to be called out and condemned.

What could be clearer than that?

But I digress. I sold out to the FBI, and whatever good I might have done to stop the war I didn't do. I was never, however, pro-war. I never had an iota of trust in the war policy of Johnson and Nixon. Especially Nixon. Johnson blundered into it. Nixon used it. Half the Americans who died in Vietnam died on Nixon's watch, in the course of his implementation of his campaign promise that he had a secret plan for peace, which he did not have (which he kept hidden). I don't see how he can be forgiven for that.

Which is to say that I entered the living room of the townhouse and greeted the collective of Weathermen with sympathy in my heart, but with a job to do. I nodded to them and started talking. "I want to get your view on how best to stop the war," I said, with pen and pad in hand.

"Elect Eugene McCarthy in 1968." That was pretty funny", and a few kids—they were all kids, even the ones in their late twenties, even if they were dressed like militiamen—laughed. We all got that the failure of Clean Gene was really the jumping off point for the radical anti-war movement. There was no hope left in the mainstream, except for heart palpitations for Bobby Kennedy—the night he won California—which were short-lived.

Someone else said, "Assassinate Nixon," which drew a chorus of "right ons" which I did not construe to be a reportable threat on the President's life. More like the good-natured banter that united a generation.

"Seriously...," a girl-woman said, a sturdy girl-woman wearing heavy glasses, who was an exception to my previously stated observation that Weather Women were generally lithe and athletic and under different circumstances could have been tennis champions at their country club, "...we are at the crossroads. To do more of the same is to add to the problem, not solve it."

"Why," I asked, "do you feel a need to solve the problem? Why is it your problem to solve? Millions of Americans see the problem, but they don't take it personally..."

That stopped her for a moment and caused her brow to furrow. But she recovered. "Are you serious?" she said. "You think it's okay for your country to be bombing babies in your name? You think it's okay to sit back and do nothing while thousands of innocent civilians are killed? There's blood on the hands of every American who doesn't rise

---

11   i.e., we were living in 1970 at the time.

up to stop the carnage...If you aren't part of the solution..."

Another woman joined in, this one more in the mold of the tennis player with good breeding. "Mr. Cox, some of us think the best way to stop the war is to bring it home to America—to show Americans the damage that bombs do to people. To put carnage in the face of Americans so they can't just change the channel..."

"Are you saying" I asked, "that you advocate, or that some of you advocate, violence against people?"

She looked at me with determination, as she might have looked at her opponent at deuce late in the match. "I am saying," she said, "that we are pushed to extremes by the fascist regime. I hate violence. We all hate violence. But violence is the coin of their realm. It's the only thing they understand..."

A guy who looked like a Che Guevara impersonator was less sanguine. "Linc, we're wrestling with methods of protest. We have options on the table. But speaking for myself, violence to people is not something I can tolerate..."

"Bill," the woman who said she hated violence said to the Che impersonator guy, "you frustrate me. I think you're part of the problem..." Her point was seconded.

My interview was not the only thing going on in the townhouse. There was flow in and out of the room, chatter in other rooms, clatter up and down the stairs, clanging and banging rising from the basement, and the aroma of oatmeal cookies wafting in from the kitchen. Not too far from a dormitory bull session, not that I remember smelling oatmeal cookies in any dormitory I resided in.

Which is when to my dropped-jaw surprise, Samantha Victor arrived. "Hi Linc," she said, giving me a smile and a wave, and squeezing herself into a place on the couch across the room from me, sort of downplaying our relationship I thought.

"Samantha, good to see you."

"You too Linc."

She looked fresh as a daisy, like she had just showered and brushed out her hair. I imagined her body smell. She wore a plain white sweater and jeans. She furled her parka at her feet. She was just twenty-one years old at the time. She glowed. I assume you know how I felt.

The generally accepted explanation for the townhouse explosion was that the Weathermen were careless and inexperienced with explosives. I didn't get down to the basement where the bomb making was supposedly happening so as to report on the safety protocol employed down there, but I can report that there was smoking going on above the basement, with the usual risk of holes burnt in the rug, conflagration of the drapes, spontaneous combustion of smoldering butts in the ashtrays, etc. Not quite the precautions you would want in a house full of dynamite.

And speaking of carelessness, here's the denouement. I passed a trash basket in the hallway on my way back from the bathroom—I didn't have to go to the bathroom, I was on a snooping expedition, which was part of my instructions—in which I saw crumbled up napkins and newspapers and, as I subsequently reported to my superiors, two sticks of red dynamite with fuses protruding like straws. "Holy shit," I almost shrieked out loud. The light was dim in the hallway, and obviously I couldn't pause to bend down to get a closer look, but I was pretty certain of what I had seen, two sticks of red dynamite nestled among napkins and newspapers in a hall trash basket. Shocking and crazy that they should be there, completely inexplicable, but in prosecution circles they would call those sticks a smoking gun.

With some difficulty I kept a poker face on my way back into the living room.

In retrospect, the Weathermen in that townhouse were kids, kids living large, kids playing at being soldiers, kids under the influence of cowboy movies every Saturday afternoon where violence led to justice and the triumph of the will of the good guys. And they were kids who trusted other kids, such as myself. They were all my friends when I left. I got a casual wave from Samantha as I reached the door, which one side of my brain tried to construe as a sign that she loved me and would always love me, and the other side took as a wish to put distance between us, a wave in lieu of a kiss, hug, or other physical proximity, like a sign saying "Keep Off The Grass." I gave a complicated, double-sided wave back to her.

We followed spy craft rules for my return to the stake-out house. I walked far from the scene, east to 5th Avenue, then south five blocks to Washington Square, which in those days you may recall was a hippie carnival every day and night featuring Bob Dylans, Ritchie Havenses, Judy Collinses, Hari Krishnas, purveyors of drug paraphernalia, hawkers of underground newspapers, dealers of pot, pamphleteers against the war, spaced out runaways, spaced out NYU students, spaced out tourists, sharing space with shadowy remnants of the pre-Aquarian underclass (i.e., bums, drunks and people talking to themselves), and parasites and denizens of all stripes and persuasions, what they called a Happening but switched to calling a Freak Show.

When I emerged on the far side of the Square, I walked crosstown two blocks to 7th Avenue where I entered the designated parking garage, walked up three flights, and jumped into the back seat of a waiting car. The windows were tinted, but I disguised myself anyway with the big hat and high-collared coat which were there for me. I was driven to the rear of our stake-out house, and rushed in through the back door and up the back stairs to the third floor apartment (the spy craft protocol purred like a well-lubed, old-fangled machine) where I was given a returning hero's welcome.

Firm handshakes all around. "Good work, kid," said Barry Flynn our team leader.

Barry, Bill Flynn his supervisor from Washington, and Mr. X—a new member of the team who was not introduced to me by name—escorted me to the breakfast nook in the rear of the apartment for a debriefing, which lasted two hours, four times longer than I was actually in the Weatherman townhouse. I described everything that I saw and heard, and then went over it again from the top. They each had a pad of paper and took notes. I was also tape recorded (on a clunky box tape recorder, of the same model I had carried with me to the Columbia U. meeting, that would make you laugh at its clunkiness if you saw it today). As you might expect, they were especially interested in the dynamite sticks I reported seeing in the hallway, and tried hard to draw a more particular description from me. But since I didn't pause to investigate the wastebasket and the sticks, and knew nothing about dynamite packaging, or dynamite debris, I didn't have useful details to draw on. "Sounds to me," Mr. X said without smiling, "that you may be describing large Coke cups, with straws sticking out."

"No, I'm pretty sure it was dynamite."

"Smoking gun," one of the Flynns said.

"Bingo," said the other.

Mr. X remained skeptical. He opened a large black briefcase, more like a combination briefcase, toolbox and arsenal, with elaborate locks, from which he pulled a pack of pictures of various dynamite-looking sticks, homemade and otherwise, and asked me if I could identify the sticks I said I saw. I picked a picture that looked close to what I had in mind. He grunted, inscrutably.

I didn't see a need to de-brief about Samantha. I described the others, however. Mr. X obligingly pulled out a pack of pictures of Weathermen, mug shots taken when they were arrested in Chicago during the Days of Rage, interspersed with high school graduation pictures which were sort of poignant considering how clean cut and bright-eyed they looked in high school before they loaded the weight of the War onto their shoulders, and grew facial hair, those who could, and donned combat fatigues. After I'd ID'd as best I could, Mr. X asked, "What about your former girlfriend, Samantha Victor?"

"Oh...yes, she was there too, I think."

"Is this her?" Mr. X asked, holding up a picture, an action shot of Samantha wielding her baseball bat.

"Yes, I think so."

Mr. X gave another grunt. The Flynns nodded.

This was a little awkward, since I might have looked less than forthcoming regarding Samantha's presence. Like I had a divided loyalty. We all lit up. Turns out Mr. X was a Camel guy, like me.

"Camels," I said to him, to acknowledge our bond.

He squinted, I think more in response to smoke drifting past his eye than to my camaraderie. He was a skillful smoker, evidenced by his ability to handle papers with both hands while dangling his Camel from the left side of his mouth in such a way that most of the smoke drifted away from his eye, and the rest was mitigated with his practiced squint, which nowadays is an extinct skill set except in select European capitals.

The moment of discomfort passed, and/or was filed for future reference.

Mr. X put a lay-out plan of the first floor of the townhouse on the table. "Where was the parlor?" he asked. I took a minute to get my bearings with the plan, then pointed to the parlor. "Where was the dynamite?" I located that too. "Did you get a look at the stairs to the basement?"

"Not really."

"Did you get a look at who came up from the basement, and who went down?"

"Not really." I got the impression that there was more FBI surveillance going on than I was aware of.

When they were done with me, Barry Flynn thanked me again— "Good job, kid"—and told me to grab a cold one from the fridge and relax. "Your work is probably done, but I want you to stick around in case something comes up. And I don't want them to see you walking around the neighborhood."

"What's going to happen?" I asked.

"It's fluid," Bill Flynn said. "We'll keep you in the loop..."

Which I completely doubted. I mentioned that the Weathermen in the townhouse looked grimmer than they had looked back in December and October. Well, the FBI guys, including Mr. X wherever he was from, looked a whole lot grimmer themselves, a whole lot grimmer on Thursday than they had on Wednesday. Something was cooking.

I got a beer, not that I loved beer—pot was my inebriant of choice, but was not well understood by my FBI colleagues at the time, and not stocked in the fridge at their stake-out—but I figured I could use a beer especially since my hands started shaking when I had a minute to myself to reflect on what I was doing and who I was doing it with and to. Again, I'm not looking for sympathy. I made my choice. Under duress, I would argue, although I don't know if you or a jury would buy my defense.

I wish I'd been tougher in the face of the FBI's overtures—closer say to Stan, the purged Weatherman, who just said "no." I wish I wasn't so quick to assume that the FBI would ruin my life if I declined, or so narcissistic to think my life was so important. But if the jury convicted me, I'd live with it. I'll just try to arrange for more backbone in my DNA in my next life.

There was a small unoccupied back bedroom. I occupied it. I lay across its bed and turned on its TV. I had schoolwork with me, a collection of poems by the poet Robert Lowell who was a big fish in the poet pantheon in those days, and may still be for all I know, although he's since died, and may be forgotten. I could read him, as long as I didn't have to understand him. The TV was more attractive.

Today's weekday afternoon TV is a smorgasbord of delights, assuming you have a good cable package. News, sports, and movies galore. It's entertaining enough to just go up and down the program pole. In 1970 there was nothing to watch except soaps. Horrible, soggy, soapy soaps with organ music which made my skin crawl. I remember laying there on that bed in that back bedroom on that Thursday afternoon with that fucking organ music playing, knowing I couldn't leave the premises, knowing I couldn't contact anybody, not knowing what was being planned by the Weathermen in the nearby townhouse or by the FBI in the rooms around me, and feeling like I could have used something better on TV.

I fell asleep thinking how nice it would have been if Samantha and I had run off to an island, she with gardenias in her hair, me chopping coconuts with my machete, the waves rising and falling along the beach.

HOPE DURANGO DID HER BEST TO BUCK ME UP AFTER
DR. FEATHER'S ANGRY DEPARTURE FROM THE STARBUCKS ON
WEST 81ST. "What does he know, that fat-nosed blowhard?"

But I knew and she knew that he knew the truth. Someone had
called him to tip him off. Someone out there was my enemy and was
spreading vicious truths about me. "How about another coffee while
we think this thing through?" she asked. "My treat."

"Fine."

I stared out the window at New York passing by. It was sunny
and cool, but not cold. Many of the passing girls anticipated spring.
Visible knees, shorter jackets, that kind of inclination. Hope returned
from the bar with the coffee, and a chocolate chip cookie as a surprise.
Starbies' cookies are okay. I'm not crazy about their muffins, histori-
cally speaking.

"What should we do now?" I asked. "My book idea is poisoned.
Nobody's going to talk to me."

"Not so fast. Let's find out who's doing the poisoning. We can
make friends with him."

"That won't work."

"Maybe it will. Admit you worked for the FBI. Apologize for your
youthful mistake. It's not like you killed anybody. You lied a little. You
passed along information. They forced you to do it. Not such a big
deal in the scheme of things. Curable by truth and reconciliation..."

The problem with Hope's rosy scheme was the final chapter of
my undercover work, as it played out on March 6, 1970. "Hope, sweetheart," I said, staring deeply into the dark and steamy brew before me,
"...there may be a monkey wrench in the gears of reconciliation..."

✳

EXCEPT FOR A QUICK PEE AND PIZZA BREAK AROUND 7:00 PM,
which I only dimly recall but which left cheese and tomato stains

on my T-shirt as proof, I stayed in the back bedroom of our stake-out apartment until the first signs of light the next morning, mostly tossing and turning my way through lurid anxiety dreams— being lost, being late, being unprepared, being trapped. A couple times I thought I'd woken up, but hadn't, and was still caught in the web of the dream. At some point someone closed my door, I assume either to help me sleep or to keep me in the dark.

I was groggy and thick-headed when I was finally up and walking around. I've wondered since whether they drugged me. In this I'm abetted by rumors that the last supper of Fred Hampton was adulterated by a treacherous bodyguard so that Fred was a slow-reacting sitting duck when they came for him, although such conjecture obviously inflates my importance in the grand scheme of subversion repression. Besides, there've been many other times unrelated to clandestine activity when I've slept badly, with bad dreams, and awoke in a stupor, such as the night before the custody hearing for my boys, or the nights I start dwelling on my memories of Samantha.

I peed, brushed my teeth, and dragged a comb across my head. There was warmish coffee in a pot on the stove in the kitchen. This was long before Starbucks upgraded my coffee aesthetics. I poured myself a cup from the pot. I drank what I poured. Tasted like sludge. Not bad.

The place was eerily quiet. At first I assumed everyone else was still asleep, but as I drifted toward the front of the apartment, looking in rooms, it dawned on me that everyone else was gone. By alien intervention, mass hypnosis, or the approach of cholera—why else in the popular culture do people abandon their beds in the middle of the night? Except when I reached the front room with the view of 11th Street, there was a guy with a high-powered rifle across his lap looking out the front window, and his teammate who was watching the street through binoculars, and a third guy who was curled up on the couch with a baseball hat pulled down low, none of whom I recognized.

"Hey kid," said the guy on the couch, apparently able to see me through his visor, or because he had a third eye implanted in his neck, or maybe I was caught off-guard and struggling to make sense, "I have a message for you from Agent Flynn. He said he hoped you had a good night's sleep. He said he didn't think he'd have any more assignments for you today, but he doesn't want you wandering around the neighborhood, so he says you should stay put here until he gives you the all clear."

"Where's he?" I asked.

"Go to the window."

I did.

"Do you see the rental van down there, the U-Haul, across from No. 18..."

I nodded.

"He's in the back of it..."

"Why..."

"It's a special van..."

"What? What's going on?"

"We're going to have a big bust..."

"Oh." A bunch of thoughts occurred to me, including that I might still be in the decompression chamber on the exit ramp of dreamland. I was not smoothly processing the information that was being served to me. "Who?"

"Whoever's lucky enough to be in No. 18 at the time..."

"What's with the rifle?"

"Plan B, in case things go differently than expected."

"Who would you shoot?"

The guy lifted his cap, and I could see his whole broad face, a friendly American face. He gave me a grin, like I'd already got whatever I was going to get from him. "We'll see," he said.

"When will this happen?"

"Kid, it'll happen when the time is right..."

I didn't ask any more questions. My mouth was dry. I thought about the possibility of a repeat of the Fred Hampton bust from a few months before. I didn't have all the Hampton facts, I didn't know the ballistic trajectories or the time sequences or anything like that, and

I certainly didn't know that after ten years of litigation the families of Hampton and Mark Clark, a Panther killed with Hampton, would settle their wrongful death civil claims against the authorities for $1,850,000. But based upon what I knew about the FBI's institutional animosity toward Hampton and the Panthers, I had trouble with the resisting arrest part of the story.

And even if there wasn't a formal plan to preemptively eliminate the risk of resisting arrest, there were many other pathways to disaster, including what either side might instinctively do as and when the shit hit the fan, or for that matter what the individual players on either side might do. It only takes one guy with a gun or a fuse to ignite a conflagration, as we've seen in hundreds of movies and television shows. I hoped for a nice, quiet, bloodless, resistance-free bust, but was deeply nervous, and could not catch my breath.

I retreated to the back of the apartment and actually thought about reading Robert Lowell as a potential nerve-calmer—the poet as out-of-the-box thinker at a time when the box felt very constricting—but I opted for the shower, the shave, the cold pizza, the drama of watching this thing play out. By then I was re-using underwear and socks, if you're interested in some of the gritty details of the stake-out. When I was all dressed and ready to go I felt stinky inside and out.

And not to dwell on Robert Lowell, against whom I have nothing but admiration for his reputation, but I did formulate an insight for life arising from his unopened poems which has served me well since, which is that I should never leave home without a low-brow novel.

I took a seat with a view of the street. I observed the U-Haul, as it sat there seemingly minding its own business, its silver roof shimmering in the sunshine of the morning. I also observed street repairs, regular old street repairs which are so ubiquitous in New York City as not to raise an eyebrow—a hole in 11th Street which I didn't recall from the day before, with steam rising out of it as always seems to be the case, and guys with picks and jackhammers standing around, and a uniformed police officer moving the traffic along.

"Is the street repair part of our team?" I asked.

"Would make sense," said the guy with the gun.

Around ten o'clock, as nothing was happening, I asked our gunman what was taking so long. He deferred to the guy who formerly was stretched on the couch, but who was now up and about, talking too quietly for me to hear into his two-way radio. When he put it down, I asked him.

"Kid," he said, "we are waiting for the meeting to begin."

"What meeting?"

"The big meeting."

"The Weathermen are having a big meeting?"

"That's the word." He gave me his no-more-questions grin.

"Oh."

I could see east on 11th Street to 5th Avenue, which was about forty yards past No. 18, and west on 11th Street all the way to 6th Avenue, about one hundred fifty yards away. 11th was an active cross street, with traffic getting backed-up to 5th on account of the ersatz street work. There were pedestrians moving in both directions. I looked for familiar faces. In the course of an hour I observed one guy and one woman enter No.18, and one guy exit, none of whom I recognized. I remember, or think I remember, that the exiting guy looked up to our window, and our guy with the binoculars nodded to him like he was someone, which really couldn't have happened because of the angle, the sightlines, and the distance, I don't think.

I considered giving Robert Lowell another shot. I considered daytime television.

At about 11:30AM, I stood up to stretch. In mid-stretch, as I faced west toward 6th Avenue, I saw Samantha Victor at the intersection of 6th Avenue and 11th Street, heading east toward me and No. 18.

You would think that after sitting around for hours doing nothing I might have developed a plan for this contingency, like Plan A: sit and do nothing while Samantha walks down the street, enters No. 18, is swept up in the bust, convicted of conspiracy to blow up America, and sentenced to jail forever, or the alternative Plan B: run to the street, head her off, and save her.

But I had nothing planned. I hadn't weighed, analyzed, or dug into whether Samantha would love me forever if I gallantly saved her, or whether the FBI would ruin me forever if I violated orders to stay put.

The guy with the two-way was talking into it with intensity. The other two were focused on the front door of No. 18. We were on the third floor. There were back stairs leading to a back alley which ran parallel to 11th Street, which was my route into the building the day before after my meeting with the Weathermen.

"I'm going to the bathroom," I said to no one in particular, thinking as soon as I said it that that was more information than anyone needed and might cause an eyebrow to raise, but no one reacted. I was immaterial. I walked to the back.

I estimated I had about a minute.

I reached the back door, out of sight to the guys in the front, and quietly turned the bolt, and let myself out onto the back stairs. I quietly closed the door behind me. I raced down the stairs to ground level, pushed open the steel door, and was in the alley. I estimated I had about forty seconds.

I ran down the alley in the direction of 6th Avenue. After sixty yards I cut left at a strip between buildings, which led me back toward 11th Street, like a wide receiver running the out part of a down and out. I reached the front edge of the buildings on the north side of 11th Street, i.e., the sideline, with no time left. I was screened by the buildings from observers in the stake-out apartment, so long as I didn't cross the sideline. I looked for Samantha. I didn't see her.

Not on the street in either direction. Not to my left, in the direction of No. 18. Not to my right, between me and 6th Avenue. I wondered if I had miscalculated entirely and she was already off the street and into No. 18. If so, should I walk to the door of No. 18 and ring the bell? Under cover of asking her out for a date? For old times' sake? That would be stupid and desperate, I realized, but I didn't reject the idea out of hand. I kept spinning what I might say to her at the door.

✸

ON THE TRAIN RIDE HOME FROM MANHATTAN WITH HOPE, FOL-
LOWING OUR SABOTAGED MEETING WITH DR. FEATHER, I duly
called in the Dr. Feather episode to Fred S—my FBI contact person.
My deal was a little like having an extended warranty on a car. They
promised to cover me in the event of a threat to my life arising from
my service to the FBI. On the other hand, they could deny coverage
if they determined that my life wasn't really in danger, or that the
trouble was my own fault, such as when you take your car to be fixed
by an unauthorized mechanic and he screws it up, or you fail to make
a claim for coverage within the warranty period.

My first meeting with Fred at my condo—the night Hope extrap-
olated my back story—largely involved just filing the claim. The car
was still drivable so no need to tow it in and replace parts just yet.
Fred gave me his direct dial number and his personal assurances that
he had seen stuff like this before and that I had nothing to worry
about, probably.

"Hmm," he said this time, when I telephoned him with my
Dr. Feather report. "This is more troublesome." He repeated the
famous Goldfinger dictum uttered when James Bond kept crossing
Goldfinger's path. Once is no concern. Twice is coincidence. Three
times is enemy action.

"Can you find out who's doing this," I asked, "and how he found
out about my FBI connection..."

"We didn't divulge..."

"I'm not accusing..."

"I've been slow-pitching the investigation, for your own good, to
keep from drawing too much attention and blowing your cover..."

"I appreciate that, I think."

"...but I'll see what I can dig up...When's your next scheduled
interview?"

"Tomorrow. At Foxwoods Casino..."

Hope whispered for me to tell Fred that she and I were now part-
nered up on the book.

"What's that?" he asked.

"Nothing," I said, worried about the fine print in the coverage exclusions.

✱

HONESTLY, I DON'T THINK I WOULD HAVE ACTUALLY RUNG THE BELL AT NO. 18, looking for Samantha. But the gravitational pull in that direction as I stood between buildings on the lip of 11th Street was compelling. Lunacy, but compelling. In the tension of the moment, she was all that mattered. I was awhirl for her in a go-for-broke adolescent way that eclipsed all cautionary constraints. I labeled it love. Love meant never having to say it's too dangerous. Love meant I didn't want to live without her, and was prepared to prove it by bearing my breast and ringing the bell. For all the same reasons why adolescents make the best soldiers, suicide bombers, and rock and roll singers, and don't give a second's thought for consequences, and a life behind bars.

But I was spared—denied—that test of my love. I spotted her coming out of the bodega at the corner of 6th Avenue. On my side of 11th. Walking toward me. My heart threatened to jump out of my chest and run to meet her.

I waited, as one might wait for one's bag as it rotates on the conveyor belt at the airport, when the bag contains contraband worth millions of dollars and the Feds are closing fast, waving guns and warrants. She had a nice natural pace. Legs and arms swinging under cover of a short coat. She held a bouquet of violet tulips which she must have bought at the bodega. She seemed to be enjoying the hint of spring in the air.

She was upon me. I reached into the sidewalk space and grabbed her, and dragged her into the alley.

With her hand that held the violets she smacked me on the side of my head. She slammed me in the chest with her knee. I held on, saying "Samantha, it's me. Samantha, it's Linc..."

"What the fuck are you doing?" she said, furiously grinding her knuckles into my forehead. "Are you out of your mind? Do you want me to call a cop..."

Which was sort of ironic under the circumstances.

"Samantha, you can't go to the Weatherman meeting. The FBI are waiting."

"What?" She looked at me uncomprehendingly. "What are you talking about?"

I held her by her shoulders. Her face was just inches from mine. Our eyes met. I pursed my lips. She bashed my jaw with her head like it was a hammer, and writhed violently to break my grasp.

"Samantha...The FBI are..."

And that was when No. 18 exploded. A huge kaboom. The shock wave drove us into the brick side of the building, body to body.

I closed my eyes and held on for dear life.

I might have lost consciousness. The next thing I remember I was on the dirt. Samantha was free of me, standing on the sidewalk watching the flames shoot out of No. 18. My ears rang, which was partially attributable to the sirens of approaching emergency vehicles.

Samantha looked down at me, but didn't speak. She walked away in the direction of 6th Avenue.

PART II

I TELEPHONICALLY REPORTED TO FRED S—my FBI contact—on my unpleasant meeting at Starbucks with Dr. Feather—the ex-Weatherman with the big puffy nose. Then I nestled into Hope and closed my eyes as our train rumbled back to Connecticut, and gave her the story of the last minutes of my FBI work on March 6, 1970, from the time I saw Samantha Victor emerge from the bodega on 6th Avenue with flowers to the time shortly afterwards when I saw her turn on her heel and go back to from where she came as flames shot out of No. 18.

"You saved her from getting blown up," Hope said.

"Yes, I think so. I mean assuming no intervention by me, and that she kept walking to No. 18 at a steady pace, with no pause for small talk with passersby, no dog incidents or twisted ankles, or other detours or delays, and assuming that her arrival there did not somehow affect the outcome..."

"...Like how?"

"...Well, I'm just saying that she was a variable, and while I don't think her reaching No. 18 would have changed the course of events, it is possible that the FBI would have given the delay signal if they were trying to figure out who she was..."

"...assuming it was the FBI who blew the place up..."

"...Yes. Right. If it was the Weathermen who blew it up, I don't think she would have caused things to change, except that it is possible one of the guys playing with dynamite in the basement might have come upstairs to open the door for her rather than use that time to connect the wrong wire..."

"...So assuming the same time of explosion..."

"...Yes, assuming that, I calculate she would have been inside the townhouse, taking off her coat, and looking for a vase for her tulips..."

"Linc, I think you saved her life." Hope was big on silver linings. She was a natural sunny-side-upper. "Do you think she saw it that way?"

"She's had some years to reflect on it. Maybe..."

"At the time?"

"I think she thought I knew the FBI was going to blow the place up, and hated me for it..."

"Did you think the FBI was going to blow the place up?"

"Do you mean before the place blew up did I think the FBI was planning to blow the place up?"

"Yes."

"I thought that might happen, and I also thought they might go in for a bust and shoot the Weatherman in self-defense. In the lead up there were all sorts of intense conversations going on among the hard guys in our apartment. I told you that we had bomb specialists from the beginning, and one guy whose skill was to break in from under the street and was pushing for that. I didn't know what they might do. I was..."

Hope gave me a classic therapeutic nod of sympathetic encouragement, including a hint of moisture in her eyes. She was adept at drawing me out.

"...very concerned. So when I ran out to stop Samantha..."

As I spoke the thing played again in my head, across a field of forty years, me running down the stairs and through the alley, running against the clock. Me confronting Samantha. Needing to rescue her. Rescuing her was more important than all the other things put together.

"Samantha," I said, as though I was speaking to her that day on the street. "Don't go there...Don't..." *Kaboom.*

After a respectful pause Hope asked, "...At the time of the

explosion, did you think the FBI did it?"

"...Of course."

"...Do you still think so today?"

"...I don't know. It sounds so wacky and extreme..."

"...Back then the FBI was scared of armed insurrection by radicals..."

"...I know. The radicals were the jihadists of their day. Maybe not as alien as the Panthers, but bad guys. Dirty and subhuman. Expendable."

"...So maybe yes?"

"...Yes, maybe..."

"...Did you ever think the FBI could have fucked up, and inadvertently connected the wrong wires?"

"...No one says they were infallible. But I will say they were pretty fucking good with bombs, and explosives and electronic devises. My guess is that if they caused the explosion, they meant to cause the explosion."

"...A direct order from J. Edgar?"

"...My sense is that if you're a true believer you don't need to hear God's voice to know you're doing God's work. It's instinctive. That could be what killed Fred Hampton."

"...Abu Graib?"

"...Whatever. There's lots of examples of lower level guys taking the bull by the horns and dragging it down the street..."

"...But you don't think Samantha was thankful to you for saving her life?"

"...I think she thought I was part of the murder of her friends. And she wasn't thankful for that."

"...Sometimes you can only save one person, and that's the best you can do."

"...Maybe she thought that...But I doubt it."

"...What if it had just been a big bust, and no explosion, and that's what you saved her from..."

"...Maybe different."

"...Is she why you're doing the book?"

"...What do you mean?"

"...To find her and apologize to her."

"...No."

"...To rekindle the love?"

"...No, that would be crazy."

✳

I SAT SLUMPED AGAINST THE WALL IN THE SPACE BETWEEN BUILDINGS OFF OF WEST 11TH STREET. Akin to shellshock, of the psychological kind although blood was dripping from my forehead from hitting the wall or getting hit by Samantha or whatever. I was woozy and slow, and hearing a lot of bells ringing.

With difficulty and disorientation I stood up and shuffled back to the stake-out apartment. There was chaos across the street, where No. 18 used to be. Flashing lights of every color, sirens of every decibel, firefighters, cops, gas men, ambulance guys, photographers, gawkers, a flamboyant contingent up from Washington Square, everybody in the world except no one I recognized from the FBI. They had cleared out. No U-haul. No street workers. Nobody in the apartment to buzz me in.

An EMT positioned along the fringe spotted my bleeding head, and sat me down for clean-up and bandaging. She asked questions, but wasn't pushy about receiving coherent answers. She said I should take a stitch or two, and that my eyes looked overcast and cloudy. She recommended I go to the hospital. I declined. As a result I have a small scar above my left eye which reminds me of March 6, 1970 every time I look in the mirror, although over time there's definitely been fading of the scar if not the memory.

I mumbled my thanks to the EMT. I padded away from the scene like the old red fox I once saw whose den had been washed away by huge rains. He moved dazedly past me toward higher ground.

Life was clumsier, totally inefficient and disgustingly dirty in the days of phone booths, before cell phones. The receiver was always battered from hard use and vandalism, and sticky to the touch. You needed change which I never had. You might be standing in some-body's pee. You had to dial 411 to get a telephone number, instead of just zipping down your hand-held digital memory bank. Instead of calling to where the person you wanted to talk to was, you called to a place where he used to be or was headed to but hadn't arrived at yet. Message machines were a thing of the future. The call kept ringing in space. Or else the line was busy. Can you remember the annoying sound of a busy signal?

Except in my state of disorder, after I'd drifted a couple blocks uptown, I settled in for rest and rebooting in a phone booth with a seat. It was available. There was no entry fee. I appreciated the shelter (my fellow exile, the dazed old red fox, might have felt the same way if he came across an uprooted stump with a cozy opening). I could still hear sirens, but they weren't my problem. I closed the booth door, closed my eyes, and dropped out.

When a guy tapped on the door a while later, to see if I was alive or to use the phone, I was recuperated enough to wave him away, and try to remember my emergency number.

On the second try I dialed it right—do you remember the slow-ness of the dial, as you dialed it forward and it rewound backward clack-clack-clack-clack in its own sweet time—and connected to Cheryl, secretary to Bill Flynn, my team leader, although by then as the internal shit was hitting the fan he might have already been my ex-team leader. "Please tell him I'm okay, and I'm going home."

The rest is history.

I wasn't reimbursed for my dirty laundry—dirty socks and under-wear, as opposed to nefarious deeds—which I'd left behind, along with my toothbrush and my book of Robert Lowell poems. I never saw those poems again.

I don't think anybody knew I was AWOL from the apartment at the time of the explosion, or at least no one has ever confronted me with that accusation. In the panic that followed the explosion it was every man for himself. To the extent anybody thought about me while running for the back alley themselves, I wasn't a priority.

Back in Cambridge that night—via the train—I thought I was okay, but I wasn't. I climbed into bed and stayed there the rest of the night and all of the next day and night, listening to rock and roll on the radio, except for meals and except that in the wee hours of the second night I ventured out for a walk along the river, which in those long ago days was a popular activity. The riverbanks were crowded with moon-eyed drifters. There was a sense that the old way was rapidly changing, including the old way of sleeping at night and staying awake during the day.

I'd blown off my homecoming meeting with Mike my handler, which miffed Mike. He tracked me on my walk, and stepped out of the shadows along a dark stretch of river.

"Kid, what the fuck is going on with you?"

"With me? What the fuck is going on with the FBI?"

"We're still open for business, kid. You have a question, you ask it..."

"Okay, tell me what went down at the townhouse?"

"I can't talk about that..."

In those days the river was deeply polluted, and often stank. Raw sewage flowed into it via discharge pipes from miles of abutters who had always done it that way. Condoms, carcasses, and crap floated on the surface. A guy I knew swam across it on a bet, and was in the hospital for a week with weird infections. I stared into the body of the river as its dirty fingers rippled near my feet. "Mike," I said, "my newspaper thinks I'm writing a story about the explosion."

"You can't do that. Your involvement is a very non-public subject."

"Not focused on my FBI involvement. As a journalist, doing investigative reporting..."

"I don't think so..."

"My newspaper knows I was in the townhouse the day before the explosion..."

"How so?"

"A Weatherman who was in the townhouse when I did my interview—lucky for him not to be there when the place blew up—turns out to be a friend of a friend of my editor..."

"...Give me their names..."

"...and word got back to my editor that I was in the townhouse and writing a story. She called to find out how many words and when will it be done. She says it sounds great. A potential Pulitzer."

Of course, what I told Mike wasn't true. It could have happened that way, it just didn't. I'm the one who told my editor I was in the townhouse, and I'm the one who said it sounded like a potential Pulitzer. My editor is the one who said it sounded like a problem.

"How the hell did you know the Weathermen were in the townhouse?" she asked me. As I worked out my answer to that one, she added, "Do you realize the FBI is going to be on your ass if they find out you were in the townhouse? Holy shit, I've got to call the lawyer."

I started having trouble keeping my stories straight.

Mike said, "I don't want you writing this story."

"I have to, Mike," I said. "They already think I'm writing it..."

"The text will have to be approved..."

"Getting approval of my writing is not part of my deal."

"Yes, it is."

"No, it isn't."

"Kid, you've developed an attitude problem."

The next day I had downtown meetings with the newspaper's lawyer and with the FBI's attitude evaluator. Their offices were a block apart. I kept the duplicative cab fare. The lawyer said that if the FBI found out I was in the townhouse they would threaten me with conspiracy charges, and try to turn me. "I don't believe that," I said.

The attitude evaluator wanted to know if I was smoking dope. "Aside from it being against the law, it helps you make bad decisions."

Both meetings ended inconclusively, as far as I could tell. After the lawyer warned me about the FBI trying to turn me, I asked him hypothetically what would happen to a person who faked being turned by the FBI, and then spilled the beans on them. To which he shook his bushy head, and said, "Lincoln, it might be a fascinating court case, but I can almost guarantee that this hypothetical person you speak of would be ruined. The government plays by its own rules when it comes to protecting its secrets. No Constitutional principle is sacred. Don't believe what you read in your textbooks..."

The FBI's attitude evaluator offered similar advice. "Lincoln, the FBI is your friend, and will always be there for you. But this friendship requires you to play by the rules, and not change the rules in the middle of an assignment. If you want to go off half-cocked and write stories about your FBI experience..."

"...I never said that..."

"...that would be regarded as a serious breach of the rules..."

"...I never said that's what I was going to do, but what if I did?"

"...Lincoln, if you were to write something that would be damaging to national security, countermeasures would be taken..."

"...But I didn't agree to not talk..."

"...Countermeasures and consequences..."

"...I..."

"...Are you familiar with the Espionage Act of 1917?"

"...No..."

"...It says we have power to protect ourselves..."

Reader, you may remember Daniel Ellsberg? He was important and famous to the antiwar movement. In a dark time, when Nixon seemed to care more for preserving and protecting his power than in preserving and protecting the Constitution, when his stated reasons for continuing the Vietnam War sounded self-serving and duplicitous, and when opponents of his war policy were labeled as traitors, Ellsberg was a bright light. He is or should be in the top ten of my generation's mainstream heroes—along with John Lennon, Bob Dylan, Gene McCarthy, J.D. Salinger, the Smothers Brothers, Woodward and Bernstein (when they were young), Peter and Jane Fonda (intermittently), Jack Kerouac, Timothy Leary (borderline), Mohammed Ali, and Norman Mailer (at the time of *Armies in the Night*). Anyone else?

Ellsberg was a Fifties-style Cold Warrior, a trusted agent of the military industrial complex who lost his faith, and at great personal risk went public in June, 1971 with a collection of top-secret government documents called the Pentagon Papers which exposed hypocrisy, lies, and unworthy arrogance of the war-makers. He was prosecuted under the Espionage Act of 1917. It is said that he expected to go to jail. Except that in a turnaround anticipatory of how Weathermen Ayers and Dohrn went free, the judge dismissed the charges on account of gross government misconduct, to wit illegal wiretapping of Ellsberg, and a notorious break-in at the office of Ellsberg's psychiatrist in an effort to discover dirt to discredit him with.

The unpleasant truth that emerges from the Ellsberg story is that facts don't influence political opinion. Those who supported Nixon and the War reacted to Ellsberg's disclosure in kneejerk fashion by condemning the messenger, and demeaning without refuting the content of the Pentagon Papers. They continued to support Nixon and the War. Those who opposed Nixon and the War proclaimed the victory of their preconceived notions of governmental dishonesty, but failed to gather substantial new popular support. They continued to wring their hands while Nixon won the 1972 election in a cake-walk. These reactions suggest instinctive tribal loyalty rather than the informed consent of an educated populace. Nobody has an open mind, and you can quote me.

I was a year before Ellsberg, and didn't have the benefit of learn-ing from his gauntlet of coming out experiences. Had I known how the government would go after him, seeking to bury him and spread salt on the ground above his grave (metaphorically speaking), I might have been more cautious. On the other hand, had the government known about Ellsberg in my year, and what a resourceful pain in the ass he seemed to be, I doubt they would have let me get within an arm's reach of a typewriter.

And on the third hand, I don't claim Ellsberg's altruism or courage. I was torn up inside by what happened at the townhouse. There was blood on my hands I couldn't wash off. But what pushed me out of my hole and to my typewriter was that Samantha—the one person in the world I loved (let's call it love, where's the harm?), and would do anything for—hated my guts. And would hate my guts forever unless I did something about it.

HOPE AND I LEFT HER CAR WITH THE FOXWOODS VALET, WHO
WISHED US GOOD LUCK.

We were a few minutes early for our scheduled 3:00 PM meeting
with Albert W, a Weatherman who was arrested for conspiracy to riot
in the Days of Rage. The judge dismissed the charges when Albert
enlisted in the army. Albert was a high-principled guy. He hated the
War, but it bothered him that the guys who fought and died in it were
overwhelmingly poor, were drafted or enlisted out of high school,
didn't have the chance at college student deferments or the resources
to establish obscure deferrable medical conditions. Rich and privileged kids tended to find a way out.

Albert had outs, including another year of student deferment
if he could convince his dean to take him back despite a record of
on-campus trouble making. But Albert couldn't stand that if he took
the deferral, some poor kid would stand in his place in the rice paddy,
and take his designated bullet. So Albert enlisted.

Albert wrote about his decision to enlist, and about his experience in the army, in an article in a national magazine circa 1980, which
you can google. I read it at the time. It made a blip, but dropped off
the screen because, I guess, it was preaching to the choir, and was
unwelcome information along the lines of football concussions and
low sodium diets to everyone else. He retired as a high school math
teacher last year, which allowed him more time and a full pension to
utilize in pursuit of his born again calling as a hold 'em poker player.

Hope and I wended our way through the casino to the poker room,
which was as big as a football field and sounded like a country night
in August with a full orchestra of crickets chirping like mad—a field
of poker guys playing with their chips replicates a lovely moment of
reflection and intimacy with nature. Click-click-click-click times a
thousand.

I spotted Albert with stacks of chips in front of him, and a mess of
chips in the middle of the table. Utilizing my education in the game,

acquired over time by arduous study and costly tuition payments, I sized up that two players remained in the hand, Albert and an old timer with flowing white hair under a golf hat who had just raised. Albert stared at the old timer, stared at the shared cards, stared at a passing cocktail waitress, and was in no hurry at all. One could hear the ticking of an imaginary clock as Albert ground out his analysis. The old timer broke the silence. "What'll it be, Albert?"

Apparently this was the sign Albert was waiting for. He pushed his chip stacks to the middle of the table and calmly said, "All in."

Now it was the old timer's turn to be the drama queen. He slowly counted his chips, divided them into shorter stacks and counted them again, took a look at his cards, took a look at the heavens, took a look at Albert, a long look like he was examining Albert for pock marks and wrinkles in addition to telltale winces and squints. "Albert," he said, "you're betting like a big shot..."

Albert said nothing in reply, with his mouth, his eyes, the color in his cheeks, the rate of his pulse, nothing that I could see to reveal his inner wish for the old-timer to call or fold. Nothing that is until his nostrils suddenly flared, which I took as an indication of aggression or else a sign that he was having trouble getting enough oxygen, or as a sign of strength or else of weakness, or as an involuntary recurrence of a known tell or an intentional manipulation of it. Now this was poker!

The old timer paled. For whatever reason, based upon whatever instinct or calculation, he could not call. He mucked his cards, threw them face down onto the felt, surrendered in the face of Albert's flared nostrils. Albert smiled as he gathered in the chips, either to say "Phew, I bluffed my way through that one," or "Shit, I overplayed it, because I so wanted you to call..."

"Hey, Albert," I said. "It's Linc and Hope. Is this a good time?"

*

THE MECHANICS OF WORD PROCESSING IN 1970 WERE CLOSER TO HOW THINGS WERE DONE IN THE DARK AGES THAN HOW THEY'RE DONE TODAY. In the Dark Ages writers wrote by hand, pen on parchment. In 1970, I wrote and edited my articles and papers by hand, pen on lined notebook pages, scratching out, scratching in, and only after I had scratched my way to a modicum of coherence or had run out of things to say did I type what I had into my Smith Corona portable typewriter, which had no facility for cutting, pasting, or any other of the magical editorial tools which are inherent in today's digital word processing. I was a fast and accurate typist by the standards of the day, but those were the skills of the archer or the swordsman compared to the killing efficiency of the remote-controlled drone.

I returned from my downtown meetings with the lawyer and with the attitude evaluator to my Harvard dormitory—think of a stately red brick country manor in the Anglophile tradition, with an internal quadrangle large enough to accommodate a pep rally or a croquet tournament—in the late afternoon, armed with a fresh pack of Camels and a back-up typewriter ribbon. My room was a second floor single, not unlike a small studio apartment. Although (not that I'm a frenetic booster), small at Harvard would be extravagant most anyplace else. No roommates and a private bathroom, for starters. I had a view of the internal quadrangle from my desk, and of the street from my bed.

There was a stair landing outside my door, with a stairway that led up to rooms on the third and fourth floors, and down to ground level, and further down to the basement which had washing machines and a pool table, and extended beneath the whole of the building so that one could enter the basement from my stairwell and resurface at the front door to the quad, if it was raining hard or if one had to smuggle a girl in or out, back in the days of girl smuggling.

I sat down at my desk to compose, old school pen to paper, not consciously clear on where I was going with the FBI's involvement in my life and in the lives of the Weathermen, but soon realizing as my pen dipped into the juice of the thing that the FBI's involvement was my story, my whole story and nothing but my story. I began, "I was recruited to work undercover for the FBI in opposition to the anti-war movement..."

I wrote with a fever through the evening and into the night. Halfway through my pack of Camels I switched to typing. By dawn's early light I rested my fingers, with ten pages of bare-breasted confessional prose stacked in front of me. In the final paragraph, the townhouse exploded and the FBI ran for cover.

Good. Nicely done, I said to myself. You've blown the whistle.

I stretched. My body was clammy, especially around my neck and under my arms. The air in the room was thick and acrid with exuded cigarette smoke. My ashtray was full and smelled like gunk. My mouth tasted like I had eaten the contents of my ashtray. I patched myself together with a hot shower, and a simulated tooth brushing (I didn't have a toothbrush or toothpaste). I dressed and walked down the stairs and across the quad to the dining hall, where I was the first for breakfast.

I had orange juice, coffee (pre-Starbies), scrambled-style eggs, buttered toast. I ate quickly and alone. I dumped my dirty dishes on the conveyor belt and headed back to my room for a good proof-reading.

I unlocked my door, stepped inside, and didn't immediately realize what had happened. The air was still smoky. The ashtray was still full. My typed pages were gone.

OMG, as the kids say. I was flummoxed, and I was fucked.

I was sure I'd left the pages on my desk, next to my Smith Corona. But maybe I hadn't. It took me a while to toss over everything that was on the floor, on the chair, mixed with my books, in and around my desk, under my bed, and run back to the dining hall on the hope that I had carried the pages with me to breakfast which I knew I hadn't.

No pages.

No credible explanation for what happened either, other than— and I found this hard to believe—a prank by my neighbor Mack who was known for his pranks. I pounded on his door. No response. Or on second thought, maybe I forgot to close the door when I went to breakfast, and a one-armed man snuck in...

"Okay already," Hope chimed in. "Cut to the chase..."

Okay. The only real decision I had to make was whether to lug the Smith Corona with me. I grabbed my innocent-looking lined notebook which they hadn't realized contained contraband notations, and stuffed it into my green bag, with underpants and socks, and a couple trinkets of sentimental value, including a photo of Samantha making a funny face, and made a run for it. Without the Smith Corona.

I got to the basement, looked both ways, and dashed for darkness.

"Were you followed?"

"It's funny what happened. The FBI got tied up in its own red tape..."

"...Funny?"

"...My handler Mike is the one who broke in and took my papers..."

"...I assumed that..."

"...He was watching my movements from a perch with a view into my room, and when I went to breakfast, he broke in to investigate. As I re-construct it, as soon as he read what I was writing, he wanted to kidnap me and ask questions later, sort of the illegal equivalent of a gag order. He called for back-up, because he didn't want to provoke a scene, or campus riot, by dragging me out in public view. His preference was to carry me out drugged and wrapped in a rug. But his request for back-up got channeled to a shift manager who obviously didn't get the memo and started asking legalistic-type questions, about kidnapping and the like. Mike got distracted, and was screaming bloody murder at this manager's intrusive protocols while I slipped down the stairs to the basement, and escaped..."

"...You're my hero..."

"...I hot-wired a car on Mt. Auburn Street..."

"...As if..."

"...Seriously..."

"...As if...Did you have a plan? Did you have a place to go?"

"...I thumbed a ride to Allston."

"...Fine..."

"...All kids thumbed in those days..."

"...I remember. We were one big, trusting, hippy generation, until body parts of girls started showing up in dumpsters..."

"...From Allston, I thumbed another ride to Brookline..."

"...Why Brookline?"

"...Brookline is where Samantha's family lived..."

"...Oh..."

"...In the estate part of town. I walked the last mile from my drop-off, up a curvy road sided by old trees and stone walls. The houses along the way were big and far apart, separated by fields. The road had bumps to deter speed and rattle intruders..."

"...Antique bumps, designed by Paul Revere..."

"...Old money bumps for sure. Nicely crumbled. Good patinas. Samantha's house was past the big bump at the top of the hill, set back from the road, a stately manse. Gravel driveway. Large rooms and tall ceilings. Imposing front entry, grand stairway inside, barn around back. It felt rich, and impervious to change..."

"...As it turned out..."

"...I know. As it turned out things change. All things change. They crumble, wither, get old, go broke, die. But at the time I admired the gentry lifestyle. I liked the promise of stability, the freedom from creditors. It looked so easy and pleasant..."

"...Creamy and dreamy."

"...Yes, it was."

"...Is that why you loved Samantha?"

"...No, or maybe, or maybe in the background. She was representative of that which was upper crusty."

"...You are such a simp."

"...True."

"But Linc, why go to her house then?"

I stared at Hope.

She stared at me.

"Hope," I said, "I went there because I liked her house. I thought maybe I could hide in the barn. I couldn't think of any other place to go."

"A hotel?"

"I didn't think of that. I didn't think of a lot of things. I was on the lam. I was discombobulated."

"...Fine. Please go on. What happened when you reached Samantha's big house?"

"...I snooped around. Utilizing my FBI training. Lurking in the shrubbery. Peering through the windows. I didn't think anyone was in the house. I took the emergency key from under the rock where they always kept it, and let myself in..."

"...Oh..."

"...I called 'hello' a couple of times just in case, and then walked up the stairs to Samantha's bedroom, which was the same as it was when we were dating, the same furniture, the same pictures, like it was frozen in time. It smelled the same. I lay down on her bed and fell asleep. With her stuffed animals..."

"...That's sort of..." Hope's voice trailed off in the dark. Her body which was curved into mine withdrew an inch or two. Her arm which was draped around my waist moved back to her side.

"...What?..."

"...That's sort of disturbing..."

✳

"YES, I KNEW SAMANTHA VICTOR," ALBERT W REPLIED TO MY QUESTION. His pockets were loaded with chips. "I ran with her in the Days of Rage." Albert, Hope and I had adjourned to a bistro near the poker room for our interview. He and I had coffees. Hope had an Amstel Light.

"Were you boyfriend and girlfriend?" I asked.

"What does that have to do with anything?" Hope interjected.

"Yes, we were, briefly," Albert said. "In the days leading up to the

Days of Rage. Which were heady times. We were taking charge of our destiny. We were planning direct confrontation. We were crossing the line, and we knew we might never be able to return, and we didn't give a fuck about it. It was an amazing, existential experience. She and I shared it, and it was quite wonderful."

I nodded, feeling how wonderful it must have been.

"Did you stay together after the Days of Rage?" Hope asked.

"No," Albert answered, "we took separate paths. I went to jail. She went underground."

I continued to nod, like a bobble-headed doll. I would have gladly smashed windshields in exchange for a day of riot prep with Samantha.

Hope asked more questions. "Did the Days of Rage work out as you hoped?"

"No. Far from it," Albert said. "We envisioned a wave of rage rippling across the United States, thousands and thousands of kids following our lead and taking back their lives and their government. But we were crazy idealists. We had no idea of what we were up against..."

"Tell me more about the week before..." I said, at the same time that Hope asked, "Do you think the Days of Rage contributed to ending the war?"

"No," Albert said in response to Hope, and maybe to me as well. "I think Nixon ended the war when it fit his game strategy. He and Kissinger viewed the war as one piece on the board, a small piece next to Russia, China, oil, nukes, and the other global shit they were playing with. My death in Vietnam was small potatoes."

"Would you do it again?" Hope asked.

"Do what again?" I asked.

Albert leaned back and pondered Hope and me and our questions. To me he said, "I take it that Samantha Victor was...important to you?"

I nodded.

He nodded.

To Hope he said, "I'm proud of my opposition to the war. I knew the war was stupid and crazy. And history has proven me right. 100%

right. It wasted the lives of 54,000 Americans, half of whom died after Nixon became president, including Chuck, Manny, and Big Joe, who were my close buddies. I don't think I should forget them no matter how much time has passed. Fuck Nixon."

As I said, Albert was a clear-thinking honorable guy. How could I hate Albert?

Let me count the ways.

✳

I SLEPT THROUGH THE MORNING ON SAMANTHA'S BED IN HER BIG HOUSE IN BROOKLINE, UNAWARE OF A BREWING FBI DRAGNET SEEKING TO APPREHEND ME AND MY REPORTORIAL ASPIRATIONS. When I awoke, with Samantha's personal smell creeping around my cranium, I felt for that brief instant, like when the quadriplegic awakes and thinks he can walk, or the prisoner awakes and thinks he is free, that I lay next to Samantha with our whole lifetime ahead of us.

"Linc, let's move on with your day."

"Okay. To my relief, or partial relief, the house was still empty."

"Partial relief?"

"I wouldn't have minded seeing her parents."

"They hated you."

"Yes, but...we could have commiserated together."

"A circle of grief..."

"A round of drinks."

"A family hug."

"More drinks."

"Watch out for the baseball bat after all those drinks."

I found a tin of saltines and a jar of chunky peanut butter for my lunch. I couldn't find a typewriter. I re-wrote the whole thing in long hand. I had my notes. I rushed the ending because I wanted to get it into the mail that day.

"Where were Samantha's parents?"

Arizona. Dude ranch. They were always going places. Especially in the cold months.

"Did you think Samantha might show up?"

I didn't know where she went after the townhouse explosion. It was possible that she might come home.

"Which was better, the first version or your new one in long hand?"

Not too much difference, except for legibility issues and a few turns of phrase which were lost and a few gained, and except that the new version included that the FBI stole my first version, which I thought was a good detail to add. I walked it down the hill, to where there was a little clump of stores. I wanted to make a copy.

"So you could mail one to the newspaper, and one to *The New York Times...*"

"I wasn't thinking *New York Times.*"

"Ellsberg thought *New York Times.*"

"He was smarter than me."

"Ellsberg also sent his to the *Washington Post* and the *Boston Globe...*"

"I ended up not making any copies because I ran out of time. In those days making copies wasn't so simple. The only public copy machine I found was in the liquor store, and it wasn't working. They posted a sign on top of it: 'Please stop kicking the machine.' And I was three blocks from the Post Office with just a few minutes to closing. I decided to mail what I had. No copy."

"Any problems at the Post Office?"

"I tried to act like I wasn't dropping off the Pentagon Papers, you know, like there was nothing interesting about my package that would make the Post Office want to open it and check for marijuana seeds, or remnants of a burnt American flag. In those days, you may recall, every interaction with the short-haired world was tipped with paranoia."

"Both ways."

"I got it mailed, then bought a submarine sandwich and soda and trudged back up the narrow road to the big house. It was dark by then, a moonless night unenlightened by streetlights. Two cars passed me *en route.* I crouched behind trees as they passed, to avoid being seen or hit. Once at the house I stumbled my way through the dark to the door. Still no signs of life. I re-entered. I was afraid to turn on lights. I ate my sub in the dark. I made calls."

"To who?"

"Whom."

"That's what I'm asking."

"I called the guy who lived across the stairwell from me, Mack, sort of a friend. 'Hello,' he said."

"Mack," I said. "It's Linc."

"Linc, where are you?"

"Why?"

"Heavy guys are looking for you. Word is that you've become a radical terrorist. Which sounds nuts. A wonk and a loner, maybe, but they're saying you've gone underground, and all this shit. They asked me if I ever saw explosive materials in your room..."

"What'd you say?"

"Not that I can recall."

"Thanks."

I recounted this episode to Hope in the dark of my condo bedroom, in the wee hours following our return from interviewing Albert W at Foxwoods Casino. When I stopped talking there was silence. She had rolled away, and I wasn't sure whether she had gone to sleep, and I was just talking to myself. "Hope," I said, "I put myself in a difficult position..."

"Then roll over on your other side."

"No, I mean..."

"I know..." She rolled back into me, her front to my back, her arm wrapped around me, her toes curled to mine, her warm breath against my neck.

"Thank you," I said.

✳

"DID YOU CALL YOUR EDITOR TO TELL HER A PACKAGE WAS ON THE WAY?" Hope asked me over breakfast.

"I did. The FBI was already there, asking questions. She was scared shitless. I said, 'It's Linc. Can you talk?' She said she couldn't."

"I said, 'I mailed you a package.' She said she couldn't hear me. I spoke louder. She hung up."

"She was my lifeline. Without her, I was out of plans and on the lam, which was crazy. I am not and have never been an on-the-lam person. The thing had spiraled out of control. I was feeling...in trouble."

"What did you do?"

"Nothing. I sat in the dark in Samantha's parent's kitchen, I don't remember for how long, until I heard a car turn onto the gravel driveway.

"Who was that?" Hope asked.

"I dropped to the kitchen floor and crawled to the nearest window. My eyes were attuned to the dark, but could barely pick out the car in the darkness. It rolled in slowly, lights off."

"Samantha's parents back from Arizona?"

"No."

"Samantha herself?"

"Good guess, but no again."

"FBI?"

"Winner. The car stopped near the front door. Two guys with flashlights—looking very FBI, and by that time I knew the look—got out. They walked past my window and around the house, like they were responding to a report of suspicious activity, checking doors, looking through windows with their flashlights, speaking in muffled tones, grinding gravel under their heavy shoes. I didn't know whether to go up or down, in or out. I stayed put, as close to invisible as I could make myself, a lump on the dark floor, mimicking a garbage bag.

Eventually they got back into their car and backed it into the surrounding shadows where they waited."

"Waited?"

"Waited."

"I thought they would break into the house."

"So did I. I thought they would break in, find me in the kitchen, and shoot me in self-defense. I was scared to death."

"What happened?"

"I waited. I didn't know what else to do. I wasn't a good fugitive. I lacked hope and courage. But at some point another car came up the driveway. I could tell from its puttering engine that it was a VW Beetle. It puttered to a stop near my window. I stayed low and listened.

Car doors opened. People climbed out. Doors slammed. I heard footsteps. I heard Samantha call, 'God damn it, where's the fucking key.'

It was in my pocket. I didn't think to leave it under the rock on my way back into the house. 'God damn it,' Samantha repeated, and at that point all hell broke loose. The FBI guys turned on their high beams and siren and rushed forward from the shadows, demanding through a bull horn that the VW Beatle people hit the ground.

'Like hell,' Samantha said. 'This is my house. Who the fuck are you?'

This I had to see, and I raised my eyeballs an eyelash above the windowsill. The FBI guys got out of their car with guns drawn. 'We're the FBI, ma'am. If this is your house, you'll have no problem from us. Just show us your ID.'

'Like hell. You show me your ID. You're the one who's trespassing.'

Samantha stood defiant and tall, hands on hips, almost unrecognizable in her disguise which was a plaid kilt, knee socks, green cashmere sweater, and penny loafers. She looked like a sorority girl, a debutante, the quarterback's date, and but for the hairy boy who lay hairy head down on the ground not far from her penny loafers, there wasn't an iota of bomb thrower about her. The two FBI guys stood with guns drawn, backlit by the lights of their car, wavering.

At this point all dogs began to bark.

I thought about running for luck out the back while confusion reigned in the front. I probably could have made it if I had run right away, but I didn't pull the trigger."

"Why not?"

"I don't know. That's who I am, I guess. Or who I was. And I had no place to run to anyway. And in a couple of minutes I lost my chance. Neighbors with flashlights congregated at the end of the driveway, wanting to rubberneck the excitement."

Hope raised her hand.

"What?"

"Did you consider that Samantha might be packing heat?"

"You don't have to be jealous, Hope. She was hot, especially in a kilt, but she was a lifetime ago. She's a distant memory. I've forgotten all about her. You're my today."

"You're so full of shit."

"No, really..."

"Finish your story."

"Samantha and the FBI guys exchanged ID's. I assume hers listed the house as her home and that she was a millionaire's daughter because the FBI guys lightened up in deference to her wealth, looks, and breeding, which they were trained to do, and sheathed their pistols."

"I thought she was wanted for something?"

"They weren't looking for her, Hope. They didn't have the dossier on her."

'Why are you here?' Samantha asked the FBI guys.

'We're looking for Lincoln Cox. We got a lead he might be coming here. Do you know him?'

Samantha frowned. 'I used to. Why are you looking for him?'

'Can't say.'

'Who gave you the lead?'

'Can't say. Who's the guy on the ground?'

'He's nobody. He just gave me a ride.'

'I'm nobody,' the guy on the ground said, raising his hairy head. I recognized him as a window-smashing Weatherman who had gone underground after Chicago. But underground Weathermen weren't on the wanted list for these FBI guys."

"They wanted you?"

"Me."

"Why did they think you might be there?"

"I'm not sure. Maybe because I carved the address into the top of my desk, something like that."

"Maybe your friend Mack?"

"Could be. He knew I had a crush on Samantha. And where she lived."

"What did you think was going to happen?"

"I was just hoping to avoid getting shot."

"They weren't going to shoot you..."

"Oh? One of the FBI guys asked Samantha about the key that wasn't under the rock. 'It's always under the rock,' she said. 'Someone must have taken...' The situation suddenly tightened. The FBI guy re-drew his gun.

'Was Lincoln Cox ever at this house?' he asked.

Samantha nodded.

'Did Cox know about the key under the rock?'

I didn't like where this was going. I didn't want to be a fugitive anymore. I was a United States citizen, with Constitutional rights, and no convictions. I mean I had convictions in terms of my philosophical and political viewpoints. I didn't have convictions in terms of my criminal record."

"Got it. Got the distinction."

"I didn't want to be a fugitive anymore."

"You weren't meant to be a fugitive."

"I took a deep breath, like it might be my last, held my sub wrapper high as a white flag, hollered to the world that I was coming out with my hands up, and did so. 'I'm Lincoln Cox. These people don't know I'm here. Please take me into custody, and please don't shoot me.'"

PART III

I WANT TO PAUSE HERE FOR A SECOND TO OUTLINE MY SETTLE-
MENT AGREEMENT WITH THE FBI. You will recall that under the
fear of getting shot I exited Samantha's Brookline manse waving my
white sandwich wrapper. They didn't shoot me, but they weren't nice
to me either. They had me assume the position, on my knees, head to
the ground. They cuffed me. They searched me. They appropriated
my wallet. "Are you Cox?" one guy asked.

"Yes," I said, "I'm Cox."

"Is he Cox?" the guy asked Samantha, whose information, on
account of her looks and wealth, he deemed trustworthy.

"That's him," she said. To me she added, "Cox, you are an asshole."

"Samantha," I said from my assumed position, chewing dirt with
my every word, "I'm sorry for everything that happened, I am truly,
truly sorry. Please believe me that I didn't know what was going to
happen. I had no clue..."

"Shut up," one of the FBI guys said to me.

"What happened that you had no clue about?" the other one asked,
as he elevated me by my arm pits and maneuvered me to his car.

"It's personal," I said.

"I don't know what he's talking about," Samantha said.

"The key to your house is on the kitchen table," I said to Samantha
over my shoulder as I was pushed into the caged back seat and cuffed
to a hook. "Samantha," I added, "I'm sorry I forgot to put it back
under your rock..."

"Cox, you're an...," she said as they slammed the car door shut. I detected an iota of compassion in her uncompleted castigation of me. Not a confession of undying love, but something to build on. Maybe. Enough to flutter my heart as we scattered neighbors and dogs at the end of the driveway and roared away into the night.

The FBI guys were giddy with their accomplishment.

"Where're we going?" I asked.

"Shut up."

"Are you arresting me?"

"Shut up."

"What are you arresting me for?"

They closed the window between the front and back seats, sealing me in and shutting me up.

At first it was clear we were heading toward downtown Boston, to what I assumed was federal incarceration and God knows what next, but then we slowed down and started to drive in sweeping circles along the edge of the Back Bay. I saw Fenway Park come and go four times, and the Prudential Tower loom, retreat and loom again. I was soundproofed from the chatter over the two-way radio, but I could see the initial giddiness of my captors turn sour as we went. Maybe a complication?

Finally we broke out of our holding pattern with a fast u-turn, and throttled southward along roadways I didn't know about. We zigged and zagged for close to an hour, emerging at the Naval Air Station in Weymouth (according to the sign above the gate), on the coast south of Boston, which was news to me. Sentries were waiting for us and waived us through. We parked on tarmac. A plane wheeled up to us. I was removed from the car, handed over to a new team of wardens and loaded onto the plane. I fell asleep, or was drugged to sleep by the snack they served me, and didn't awake until we were preparing to land on a private air strip somewhere else.

What happened, I found out later, was that I was a real legal hot potato, a challenge to the best legal minds among those few legal minds who had clearance to appraise my legalities. Arrest and incarceration in the normal course, with its problematic characteristic of due process of law, including right to counsel, right to get before a judge, right to be bailed out, was not an optimal solution as it would not gag me from spilling my beans about FBI involvement in West 11th Street. Dropping me into the Atlantic Ocean from 20,000 feet was a solution, but it offended the sensibilities of weak hearts in the group who worried that the punishment might not fit the crime, or that facts of my drop-off might leak to the press, or otherwise.

It was decided, or bungled into, as a temporary solution, that I should be flown (renditioned) to a safe house in a foreign land to give them time to figure out what to do with me, without judges and lefty attorneys making a big stink. It made sense at the time, as they say.

This temporary solution ran for nearly five years (arguably rough justice if you consider how long my sentence might have been had I been tried and convicted of attempted release of government secrets, but very, very rough). Each passing day made it harder for them to find a way out and easier for them to just let it ride. My safe house was an expansive American-owned estate an hour north of London, England, which didn't officially exist, which was used for various security-related purposes such as de-programming Russian spies, training American spies, and plotting African coups.

At first I was tied to my bed in a windowless bunker, with an actual gag in my mouth except when they took it out to grill me on why I'd chosen to turn anti-American, and why did I take a Russian history course during my sophomore year at college.

But cooler heads prevailed, or else the hotter heads got distracted by other crises, and within weeks I was unshackled and enjoying a plethora of freedoms and opportunities, including a sunny room with private bath and daily housekeeping, supervised walks in the non-restricted parts of the compound, run of the library, daily newspapers, lessons in squash and Spanish, rib-sticking food three times daily, all the Scotch I could drink, and easy conversation with my holders who were all Ivy League graduates.

Not unlike graduate school, or better.

They snatched my FBI exposé package from the hands of the mailman as he delivered it to Lori at the newspaper. It's never been seen or heard from again.

They got word to my mother that I was alive and on a secret mission. She believed them. They convinced Harvard to issue my degree, notwithstanding a few loose ends in my curriculum. They interviewed my known associates under the guise of checking my references for a job I was applying to, and then interviewed the known associates of my known associates, and so on. They triple searched my notebooks and dismantled my dorm furniture looking for evidence of contraband. They found *Playboys* under my mattress—I don't know how they got there—and my equally if not more embarrassing love poetry to Samantha. They intimidated anyone who was curious. I was effectively disappeared.

Fortunately, however, J. Edgar Hoover did not live forever. He died on May 2, 1972, precipitating panic in the highest ranks of the American intelligence community as dirty secrets once so closely held began to ooze from the grasp of his dead hand, not the least of which were details of COINTELPRO, his dark baby which I had served, whose mission was to aggressively interfere with domestic troublemakers without need to get tied up in knots by a bunch of Communist-colored legal technicalities, like search warrants and Freedom of Speech.

Incident to the post-Hoover panic, the perception of me as a *threat to national security* shifted to a perception of me as a *threat to the* FBI and to its hard-working public servants whom I might expose, and cause to be fired, sued, and indicted. They held a tiger by the tail.

They tried to re-educate me with daily one-on-ones not unlike psychotherapy, aiming for me to denounce my bad old self and be born again with truer patriotism. Ironically, the template for their re-education program was Mao's Cultural Revolution, which had won converts in USA national security for its clear-eyed willingness to attack and root out harmful, counter-productive, and degenerative thinking.

Try as I might, however, I was unable to convince them that I was safely re-educated, and that my bad conduct had been a brief fling which had fully passed out of my system and into the toilet bowl. I think they distrusted me because I'd gone to Harvard.

Their concern increased when Nixon's "plumbers" were arrested on June 17, 1972 while breaking into the Watergate offices of the Democratic National Committee—it looked to me like a textbook COINTELPRO operation.

As the full array of Nixon's "dirty tricks" was rolled out for television viewers in the Watergate Hearings during the spring and summer of 1973, you didn't need to be a Weatherman to know which way the wind was blowing. Nixon, a true friend of secrecy in government, resigned on August 8, 1974.

Free at last from the likes of Hoover and Nixon, Democratic do-gooders in control of Congress were emboldened to shake the tree. A Senate committee—the Select Committee to Study Governmental Relations with Respect to Intelligence Activities, known as the Church Committee after its chairman, Senator Frank Church (D-Idaho)—was convened to investigate COINTELPRO.

That's when my name and pieces of my story started popping up around the shredder machine, with increasing worry and frequency, and threatened to burst into somebody's career-ending scandal. They had to decide whether to (a) be patient because sooner or later I would die of natural causes, or (b) cause me to die of unnatural causes, or (c) fly me back from disappear-land and let the chips fall as they may, or (d) cut a deal.

I confess, my situation at the Estate, as we sometimes called it, after the initial scare tactics was never hellish and often merry. I was deprived of my freedom, but, to be candid, and not to be repeated, for quite a while I didn't miss my freedom, I didn't miss the revolution, I didn't miss having to figure out a career, I didn't miss hard work and deadlines, and I certainly didn't miss being a fugitive. I treated my incarceration like it was a spiritual retreat, with benefits, akin to a sanitarium, or a long vacation with lots of television.

How's this for a benefit: they trained spies, and from time to time

I was used as a guinea pig by female spies in training. Their job was to make me think they liked me, and to manipulate information out of me using their spy education in conjunction with their natural skill sets. They didn't tell me that. I figured it out after I kept getting lucky. Generally I coughed up information about my dealings with the Weathermen and the FBI, as a sign of my gratitude.

There were other inmates, or guests as we were sometimes called, many of them wanted by someone in connection with something bloody or heinous or counter revolutionary, many of them turning state's evidence and embarking on a new life with a new identity, a few on the mend from nervous breakdowns. They flowed in and out, never more than a handful, never staying long, some I was permitted to talk with and some not. My point being that in addition to my camaraderie with my Ivy League keepers, I had other stimulating acquaintances, as many as I wanted to be sure, and I rarely felt alone or isolated.

But by 1974 the barbed wire perimeter was looking less like protection and more like jail, and I was ready and willing to pick back up the pieces of my life, if I could find them. So when they approached me with a proposal for a separation agreement, in which I would release them from any and all claims, and agree not to do any more exposing, and they in turn would release me from incarceration, and pay my tuition and living expenses at graduate school, together with a stipend of $15,000/year for thirty-five (35) years or my lifetime whichever ended sooner, plus a good-conduct lump sum bonus at the end, I was prepared to talk.

"You know," I said to Paul M., the FBI negotiator they sent to negotiate a deal with me, "I'm afraid I'll be targeted by the Weathermen for being an FBI informant..." That led to a proviso including me in the protection program which they generally reserved for witness protection folks. I call, they protect, subject to the fine print, as previously discussed.

"Also Paul, I want a letter of commendation for my service to the United States the past five years, and an honorable discharge."

"We can arrange that."

"I want the annual stipend to start as of the date of incarceration."

"I'll check into that."

"I want the amount to be $20,000/year."

"That won't happen."

"Would you check?"

"Fine. But it won't happen."

"Also, what happens if, say thirty years from now, I disclose the FBI's involvement."

"We kill you."

He smiled, as if to re-assure me that he was kidding. "Lincoln," he said, "we reserve the right to prosecute you if you breach your agreement to keep quiet..."

"Prosecute me for what?"

"I don't think we want to re-hash all that..."

"Well I..."

"...and we reserve the right to take back all the money we've paid you as of that time, and stop any future payments, including the bonus, and take your firstborn as collateral..."

"Wha...Oh, another joke. Pretty funny. Hah, hah..."

"My point is that there would be serious problems for you if you breach this agreement...."

"What if someone else discloses the FBI's involvement?"

"The FBI is not going to disclose it."

"Okay, but what if somebody else..."

"I'd say—but without giving you an official opinion or a binding guarantee—that you're only responsible for you. You can't tell anybody, by any means, expressly or by implication, orally or in writing. But if somebody else starts talking, and didn't find out from you, I don't think you would be blamed, subject to review of the facts and circumstances."

"Can I tell my mother?"

"No."

"If I get married, can I tell my wife?"

"No, you can't. No exceptions."

"What if I get subpoenaed to testify?"

"You have to let us know immediately. And cooperate with us if we fight it."

"But what if you lose, and I have to testify? Are you telling me I have to commit perjury?"

"No, I'm not saying that."

"So if I'm subpoenaed, and I have to testify, then I can testify without any retaliation from you?"

"No, I'm not saying that either."

We went around the barn a few times. In the end I said I wanted to speak to a lawyer. He said, "Okay, as long as it's a lawyer we approve."

"Then he would be your lawyer, not my lawyer."

"Those are the rules."

"Fine. Send me an approved lawyer."

They sent me George A. George was an American lawyer living in London, working in private practice. He disclosed that he represented the United States in certain matters, but wouldn't tell me where, when or what. He disclosed that he had a high security clearance, and that as a condition to talking to me he had agreed with the FBI that he would not go public with the terms of my agreement or anything else about me.

"Can I trust your advice?"

"It's conflicted."

"Should I sign this agreement?"

"They had no business holding you here in detention, without charges, without a trial, in violation of your Constitutional and statutory rights. It's a disgrace. But I recommend that you sign it..."

I signed. I earned my doctorate in American history from Cambridge University (UK) in 1981. I met and married an English girl, Jill—an artist and pastry chef—the same year. We lived in Cambridge (UK), and other college towns, where I taught. We had two sons, Frank (b. 1983) and Delvin (b. 1985), which I always thought was a typo, but which Jill insisted was a hallowed family name, traceable to noble blood. We divorced in 1988, on the grounds of mutual dissatisfaction. She obtained custody of the boys, whom I love but have become attenuated from. My FBI stipend, which is paid out in monthly increments as though it were a retirement pension, and which I identified in my divorce papers and in my taxes as a retirement pension, was until recently largely diverted to alimony and child support, although given that the boys came of age and my ex snagged another husband the pay-out has recently improved.

I returned to the States in 1990, for a fresh start. I got low-pay, low-status teaching gigs in the high-ed boondocks for a couple years, but gradually made connections, developed credibility, published a thoughtful article on existential choices made by Benedict Arnold, and fortuitously landed my non-tenure track position with Wesleyan University, where I've been since, year-to-year, hand-to-mouth, meagerly supplemented by my FBI stipend, holding my breath until my lump sum bonus payment ($200,000) comes due.

✳

FROM THE TIME I RETURNED STATESIDE I TRIED TO LOCATE SAMANTHA. I thumbed through telephone directories and cruised missing person links on the web. I half-expected to turn a corner during some random search, or walk, or event, and bump into her. Sometimes the project rested on the shelf for a few months, but them on a slow Sunday afternoon I would pick it up again with renewed ardor. As I mentioned, the understory for my idea to write a book updating the lives of former Weathermen was that I thought it might lead me to Samantha, and to a reconciliation with her, and to putting my life back on the track that it was unfortunately derailed from so many years ago which I have not recovered from, obviously.

I realize this is not a healthy pre-occupation.

"Let's re-interview Dr. Feather," I said to Hope

"Why in the world," Hope asked, "do you want to re-interview Dr. Feather?"

"We need to reconcile. For the good of the book."

"He's not going to talk to you. He walked out on you. He called you a rat. He thinks you're a rat. And the truth is you are a rat."

"I have something for him."

"What, pray tell?"

"I can tell him about the FBI."

"What's that to him?"

"I think a lot. He wants to know."

"He already knows that you were FBI."

"He doesn't know what went down at the townhouse."

"You don't know what went down."

"Sweetheart, I was there. I'm soft on a couple details at the end of the last chapter. He's missing the whole black hole."

"What's in it for you?"

"It's for the good of our book."

Hope didn't press me on my motivation. I assume she figured out that the unspoken reason I wanted to get back to Dr. Feather was that he had contacts with Samantha.

"So, call him up," she said.

"No, I want you to call him up."

"If it means so much to you, then you should call him up."

"I thought we were partners on the book."

"We are, but this is sort of a side deal..."

"Please..."

I begged. He'd be more amenable to her than to me. She was our team's best foot forward. Most likely to succeed. She gave good chit chat. He liked her at Starbucks when we met. She kept company with a rat, but wasn't a rat herself. He liked her looks, I said.

She finally relented. I'm sure she felt dirty to do it, but she did it. She dialed. I prepared to listen to her end of the telephone conversation from a curled-up position on an adjacent couch.

She got his voice message. A bit of a letdown.

"Hello, Dr. Feather, this is Hope Durango. You met me at the Starbucks on W 84th Street last Saturday. I was with Cox the writer.

I'm sorry the meeting ended so badly. I thought you were a very interesting man. I wonder if we could continue the conversation. Please call me."

She left her cell number. She said it slowly, twice. She hung up.

I uncurled, and gave her a big hug for doing the deed.

Twenty-four hours later I wasn't so sure. "I think you should call him again," I said. "Please..."

"No way."

Her phone rang.

"Hello...Yes, Dr. Feather, this is Hope. Thank you for calling me back...Yes, may we meet again?...Uh, with Cox, if that's possible.... Cox the rat, yes...He's very sorry over what happened, and wants to explain...But if you...Uh, he wants to explain the FBI's role in the Greenwich Village townhouse explosion..."

I wouldn't have been so blunt about it. I would have danced around. But it worked. He booked us for a 10:20AM on the next Wednesday, in his offices on the 5th Floor of a shrink-and-dermatologist building on Broadway and 91st.

Hope and I had each done couple's therapy, not with each other—she and I were skimming too lightly to get stuck in the mud and need a tow, so far—but with our priors. From our respective perspectives we each recognized the scene in Dr. Feather's waiting room with unease. Stark, utilitarian, impersonal furniture and fixings, filtered air, an expectancy of bad things to come. She tapped her fingers and toes with discordant nervousness. I chewed my fingernails and prepared to duck if a lamp or heavy ashtray happened to be launched at my head.

Feather appeared, whooshing out from his inner office, with a professional smile of greeting centered around his large, expressionless nose. "Welcome Hope," he said, and gave me the briefest and coolest of nods. We were directed through the portal and into the sanctum. Two sturdy side-by-side chairs were waiting for us.

"I feel I should start talking about sex," I said.

Feather allowed his professional smile to wane, and a frosted glaze to wax in my direction.

"Fellows," Hope said, "I asked for this meeting. It's important for Linc, Dr. Feather. He is torn up about his past and wants to talk about it."

"Does he think he's here as a patient?"

"I did a bad thing," I said.

"You were an informer, Mr. Cox."

"Yes."

"If you were my patient, I would bring out reasons why what you did was not as bad as you think, and why in the scheme of things it was excusable. But..."

He didn't finish his sentence. Instead he looked at me with more of his frosted glaze. His contemptuous frosted glaze. His withering, contemptuous frosted glaze. His...You get the idea. He thought I was shit.

"Dr. Feather," Hope asked, pulling the spotlight back to herself, "do you know who blew up the townhouse?"

"It was an accident."

"Maybe."

"What do you mean 'maybe'?"

"Linc knows things."

"Like?"

"Like FBI involvement," I said.

"I don't want to hear your voice," he said to me.

"But..." I said.

"FBI involvement," Hope said.

"In the explosion?" he asked her.

"Yes," she said.

"What are you saying?" he asked.

"The FBI..." she said.

"I lost dear friends in that explosion," he said. "Except for a slow train from New Haven, I likely would have been exploded with them..."

"You were *en route* to the townhouse?" Hope asked.

"There was a meeting called to discuss bombing plans. I had strong thoughts..."

"Pro-bomb?" Hope asked.

"We were all pro-bomb. But the first question was about how to avoid blowing ourselves up. Our boys were careless. They left dynamite sticks in the waste basket..."

I made a mental note. And added an asterisk to it.

"And the next question," Feather said, "was about how to avoid blowing other people up..."

"Which you were..." Hope asked.

"In favor of."

"In favor of blowing other people up?"

"No, no. I was against blowing other people up. I was in the against-blowing-other-people-up faction of the pro-bomb division of the Weathermen Underground."

Hope and Dr. F were chumming right along, like old friends. I was invisible, which was fine enough, like listening to the radio. And, of course, the remark about dynamite sticks in the waste basket was highly perplexing, given my personal history with said subject matter. You may recall that I reported to my FBI handlers seeing dynamite sticks in the waste basket. I tried to avoid confrontation with Dr. F's nose. I observed the room.

"Was it majority rule?" Hope asked Dr. F. "Did you take votes on whether to kill people with the bombs?"

"We did vote on issues, but what tended to happen in those days was that when you lost a vote you accused the vote counter of being an FBI stooge, and you walked out of the room with your followers to start your own cadre in the next room. That was SOP."

"Sixties kids were spoiled," Hope said. "They didn't react well to 'no.'"

"Democracy isn't easy, Hope. Take the autocratic model, where you rig the vote, and after you win you round up everyone who voted against you and kill them."

Hope chuckled. She was having a swell time with the debonair, New York-based, big-nosed Dr F, who beamed nostril to nostril that he had elicited such a fine chuckle from good-looking (for her age group) Hope.

Happy hour, missing only the tinkle of glasses.

"So tell me," Dr. Feather directed to Hope, "about your perception of the role of the FBI in the townhouse explosion."

"Can Linc tell it to you?"

"I don't want to hear his voice."

"Isn't that a little dramatic," I chimed in.

"I don't want to hear your voice," Dr. F repeated. "You were an FBI informer. You had a former girlfriend who you claimed to love, and you used your connection to her to advance the interests of the FBI. That's despicable."

"I'm sorry. I'm truly sorry."

"Your sorry doesn't cut it.," Dr. F said. To Hope he said, "Let's move on. Tell me whether the FBI blew up the townhouse."

"Well," Hope said, "Linc has told me that the FBI was all over the townhouse. The phones were bugged, the basement was bugged. They had photographs of everyone who came and went, with bios. They knew how much dynamite was there. They knew so much that Linc is pretty sure he wasn't the only informer..."

"Why does he say that?" Dr. F asked, raising his nose querulously, like it was a gigantic eyebrow.

"I guess," said Hope, "because they knew a lot more than what he told them. And their whole thing was to infiltrate with depth..."

"Who else?" Dr. F asked.

I cut in. I couldn't stand sitting on the bench anymore. "Excuse me, Dr. Feather..."

"What does your Mr. Cox have to say to me?" he asked Hope.

"Can he speak for himself?" she asked.

"No, and I don't want to speak to him..." he said.

"I have a question about the Nyack armored truck robbery..." I said.

"Nyack? I don't know anything about Nyack...."

"Why Nyack?" Hope asked me.

"I wonder if Dr. Feather knew about Nyack."

Dr. F gave a harrumph. "Mr. Cox," he said, looking directly down the barrel of his nose at me, "my business is none of your business, but for the record, I quit the Weathermen in 1970 shortly after the townhouse explosion. I was sad and disgusted by the whole thing. By 1981—at the time of Nyack—I was a board-certified practicing psychiatrist, engrossed in a real life with real responsibilities. People did not come up to me and ask me to aid and abet their violent felonies. 'Dr. Feather,' he minced, 'we're planning to rob an armored truck at the Nyack mall. We have an opening for a good triggerman. Are you available?'"

He trumpeted another harrumph. "Mr. Cox, I read about Nyack after the fact, like everybody else. I didn't vote on it, you...insinuating little shit."

His weight shifted forward in his chair, like he was preparing to leap for my throat, nose first.

"But you have a lot of ex-Weathermen friends and patients. Did Samantha Victor know about it?"

That was the trigger. It drew Dr. F out of his chair. He rose with mad eyes, fists clenched, black wind streaming from both nostrils. "Nothing, Mr. Cox. And even if there were something, nothing for you. Who the fuck are you to ask me these questions?"

I rose to meet his aggression. Hope jumped between us, waving her arms, saying, "Boys...boys..."

"Get out of here, Mr. Cox," Dr. F said.

PART IV

"I thought we were a team," she said.

"We are a team."

"Bullshit."

We stood toe to toe in the thick of Broadway pedestrian traffic. "What bullshit?" I asked.

"That stuff about the armed robbery? That was you by yourself. That wasn't from my part of the team."

"I wanted to know."

"Bullshit."

"There's a possibility..."

"There is no such possibility."

"It could have been..."

"Linc, it could have been that dinosaurs spoke French. But it wasn't."

"I'm just exploring a possibility."

"No, you aren't. You sound like the people who say Obama wasn't born in Hawaii. You're concocting a conspiracy..."

"I was trying to elicit information for our book."

"What? Do you think I'm completely stupid? You think Feather can give you news about Samantha Victor? Tell you where she is?" By now she was screaming and drawing a crowd. My remark about trying to elicit information for our book was apparently a bit too disingenuous for her to swallow. She looked me in the eye like she was willing to call the whole thing off because I was just too much of a shmuck. *What did I ever see in you? Get me out of here...*

"Hey," I said, "let's go to Starbies for a cup of coffee..."

"Fuck you and fuck Starbies."

The thing was spiraling out of control. She was on the brink of crying. I wrapped my arms around her.

She pushed me away. But not with great vigor. Nothing like the time after the townhouse explosion when Samantha pushed me away with extraordinary vigor, and added a head-butt. It dawned on me that Hope—brilliant in so many other ways—might be soft on me. "I'm sorry," I said.[12]

Onlookers who had become engaged by our scene clapped approvingly at my apology, except for one middle-aged woman who said to Hope, "Honey, don't fall for that sorry shit."

"Teammates?" I asked.

"Okay."

"Lunch?"

"Okay. But you're still a shmuck..."

We found a quiet, pub-type place appropriate for weekday dalliances, with white cloths, napkins and little flowers in a vase on our table, and not by coincidence a full liquor license. I ordered a mid-day vodka martini, straight up with a twist. I urged Hope to do the same since I've found that martinis imbibed together can cure most of what ails a relationship, at least temporarily, which may be long enough, but she refused the cure and ordered a glass of common merlot instead.

"Are you thinking the same thing as me about Dr. Feather?" I asked.

"What's that?"

"That he's the guy who's been blackballing me."

"You mean you think he called Liz Caruso in Boston about you?

"Yes."

"And he faked a call to himself when we met him in Starbucks?"

"Yes."

---

12 Hope, I'm still sorry.

"I've thought of that."

"He's tight with Samantha. She knew about me and the FBI. I think she probably told him about it in the first place, and he ran with it."

"What's in it for him?"

"Pride, principles, ethics, loyalty to his old friends, all that shit. Some people just like to stick their noses into other people's business..."

We were, as you can hear, back on an evener keel. I ordered the featured cheeseburger and fries. Hope selected the Caesar salad with grilled chicken. My martini was smooth enough. Hope didn't waste any time getting to the bottom of her merlot. At our waiter's insistence—I know, I sound like a fucking lush—we ordered a second round.

Reader, I am not trying to justify my behavior. I believe I've made that point clearly throughout this accounting. I'm just telling the story of what happened, and I'll let the chips fall as they may, probably on my head. But I note, as an aside, that more and more I'm seeing guys and girls who were in love in high school find their way back to each other after thirty or forty years. It's not so exotic a composition.

✳

YOU WILL NEVER GUESS WHO CALLED ME LATER THAT AFTERNOON AS I WAS BACK IN MIDDLETOWN, CT PREPARING FOR MY CLASS.

No, not her.

No, not him either.

Give up?

Elizabeth Seaver Caruso called. Out of the blue, out of the zagatonic blue. You could have knocked me over with a feather when I saw her name light up my cell screen.

"Lincoln Cox?"

"Yes."

"This is Elizabeth Seaver Caruso speaking. How are you?"

"I am...ah...surprised that you are calling...The last time we spoke you were threatening to get a court order to keep me away..."

"Yes, and for good cause too. But situations sometimes change, you know..."

"That is true, definitely true. What has changed here?"

"You may recall that I am involved with entertainment law? I represent people in the entertainment field. I put together entertainment packages..."

"Okay."

"One of my clients has an artistic concept in which you and your history might be a good fit..."

"What part of my history?"

"Your history as a rat."

"I wasn't a rat..."

"Not that again, Mr. Cox."

"Okay, putting that aside for a second, what's the concept?"

"My client contemplates a rock musical about the Weathermen."

"Weathermen: The Musical?"

"Yes. Building on the success of *Hair* and *Les Mis* and *Miss Saigon*. Coming of age in the Sixties, American youth against the stone-faced military industrial complex, romantic idealism on the barricades..."

"Bombs bursting in air..."

"Yes, that's the spirit."

"The concept...takes my breath away."

"Yes. It's very heavy, and I think marketable."

"You don't feel it demeans the spirit of the Weathermen, to make them singers and dancers in a musical? The Weathermen I knew took themselves and their mission very seriously. They were religious in their fervor..."

"The musical is an expansive concept, Linc. Allows for unexpected turns. We'll be okay with it, and hopefully make a buck."

"Will it have a happy ending?"

"That's an open question. We're just getting going..."

"Why me?"

"Because there's an insidious underside to Peace and Love, and that's you.

"I'm...flattered."

"We want you to spill the beans on your FBI involvement. There's a rumor that you once tried to do so."

"Where did you hear that?"

"I've been digging. Is it true?"

"Yes, it's true. And I've made other positive contributions. I'm not nearly as bad as you think I am, if you take into account the body of my work, and not just the..."

"Well personally speaking, I think of you as a rat. But professionally speaking, I can get past that. You may be useful. Let's take a meeting..."

If you live long enough you'll see pigs fly.

Or you'll see a fat pigeon and think it's a pig.

Or you'll believe in miracles.

Or none of the above.

My point being that you just never know what's going to happen next. I hung up from Liz Caruso feeling unaccountably redeemed by her madcap proposition. A musical about the Weathermen? Based on the sordid tale of my FBI involvement? I felt she was saying it was time to forgive and forget. The war was over.

In my exuberance, I called Fred S, my handler.

"Fred?"

"Linc, how're you doing?"

"Things are looking up."

"How so?"

"They're making a musical about the Weathermen."

"Really?"

"Based on my FBI involvement. Seen through my eyes."

"No kidding."

"They may not be out to get me after all..."

"Well, that's possible..."

"...even though I've figured out who's been blackballing me."

"Who's that?"

"Eric Feather. The shrink."

"Geez, Linc..."

"He's in the center of the Weathermen émigré community. People talk to him, consult with him, confess to him. He knows everybody's business..."

"I don't know, Linc."

"Why's that?"

"I can't say."

✳

MY CLASS TOPIC WAS WATERGATE.

"Why," I asked my class, "did Nixon do the Watergate break-in?"—the break-in to the office of the Democratic National Committee in the deluxe Watergate office/apartment/hotel complex, high above the muddy and meandering Potomac River in Washington D.C., on or about June 17, 1972, orchestrated by Nixon's allies and executed by a team of former CIA guys with solid right wing credentials.

"He had to," said Jennifer along the side wall. "His character is his destiny, like Macbeth in the Shakespeare play. These guys are programmed to over-reach and self-destruct."

"Interesting," I said.

"*Hubris*," Jennifer added, confidently.

"I think he was afraid...," said Hank, one of my back row boys who tend to associate class participation with sleeping with the enemy, but who occasionally toss in a bomb, "...that the Dems had discovered the dope on the Republican's involvement with the Kennedy assassination..."

"Uh, I..."

"It shows," said reliable Larry, "Nixon's inherent distrust of democratic processes, and his belief that they could and should be manipulated. Nixon was an ends justify the means kind of guy..."

"Yes," I said. Any student of mine savvy enough to begin an exam essay with the sentence, "Nixon was a crook..." would likely get a good grade.

I was home that evening, by myself. Hope had late meetings. I was putting mayonnaise on my turkey sandwich and breezing through my day's emails. I opened an email from Liz Caruso. A follow-up to our telephone call, a preliminary description of the musical project, expressing her enthusiasm for my participation, including names and bios of interested people, some miscellaneous information. But Liz made a goof. She was so efficient that she attached a contact list.

Bingo. Eureka. Thar' she blows!

A street address in Darien, Connecticut affiliated with the initials "S.V." It might have been the home of Shirley Vilabosky, or Sheldon Valparaiso, but I only had eyes for Samantha Victor.

I think what happens in situations like this is that the voice that's supposed to warn you that you're about to do something stupid and dangerous gets taped shut and a bag is placed over its head. I was in go mode, pedal to the metal, brakes not functional.

It was a cold night in February—mid-twenties—with snow in the forecast. "All the better for camouflage," the voice which had taken over my controls said. "Just put on your heavy boots, a parka over old tweedy, and bring gloves. You'll be fine."

MapQuest is not blameless either. It was my enabler, from both a map and satellite perspective. It seamlessly brought me to the front gate of the designated address around midnight, in one of the plusher neighborhoods I've been to, as plush as if not plusher than Samantha's old-money digs in Brookline, Massachusetts. Along the way I imagined I was being followed, which I guess was my ineffectual way of hoping I'd be caught and stopped, although to my credit, if I stopped in my tracks every time I thought I was being followed I'd never get anywhere.

Snow was falling.

I viewed the front gate, made of heavy steel that opens if they buzz you in and stays shut if they don't. I observed embedded lights and cameras. Motion activated I assumed. I ditched my car up the road, on the shoulder under the concealing limbs of an evergreen, and walked back through the snow toward the gate. A four-foot stone wall fronted the property, like a sign that says rich people live here, and your presence is not welcome (you're sort of icky, as a matter of fact). It felt like it might be Samantha's hereditary kind of place.

One last opportunity to turn around before inflicting permanent life damage on myself passed without audible objection. I leapt the wall.

A Navy seal I am not. More like a fat harbor seal struggling to move on dry land. A smarter stalker would have eye-balled the landscape during daylight hours, or brought along night vision goggles, or at least a flashlight, so as to avoid stumbling through thorns, into boulders, and down artificial ravines. My groans were loud enough to disturb the peace. Snow continued to fall.

The terrain rose to the house, which was set back a hundred yards from the perimeter wall. A nine iron to an elevated green comes to mind. Protected by a water hazard, a frozen pond which I discovered as I slid across it. Lights were on in the house.

Plantings to hide behind stopped thirty yards short of the front portico, yielding to a flat grass lawn now accumulating snow. I crunched down to make myself scarce and invisible, and scampered across the lawn. It never crossed my mind what I would do once I got there.

"Stop," a harsh voice said. "I have a gun, and I will use it."

"Samantha? It's Linc..." I opened my arms for a hug.

Bang. A bullet whizzed over my head. I collapsed onto the snowy lawn.

"Holy shit," I said.

"Stay down," she said, "and crawl to the front door."

"Okay."

I crawled to the front door, and into the front foyer of the house. Like a dog (an obedient dog).

"Lie flat."

I did. Head and stomach flat on the floor.

"Put your hands behind your back."

I did.

"Linc, I've had enough of you."

"I'm sorry."

"How did you find out where I live?"

"I can't say."

She kicked me in the ribs with the toe of her sneaker. I winced in pain.

She re-asked her question. "How did you find out I was here?"

"Someone told me."

"Who?"

"I forget."

She kicked me again in the same spot.

"Please Samantha, can we talk..."

"How did you get here?"

"I drove."

"Where did you park?"

"Up the road, under a tree."

"Who knows you're here?"

That was a question that cut two ways under the circumstances. I tried to calibrate on the fly which way was worse for me, to be a lone stalker who lay helpless on her floor, or a team member stalker with reinforcements coming who lay helpless on her floor? And despite being kicked twice in the ribs, I still held out the hope that she was just playing with my head, and didn't intend to seriously hurt me.

"Hope—my girlfriend—she knows I'm here."

"Really?"

"Really. She and I are a close team..."

"You dropped your obsession for me for Hope? Poor Hope..."

"...I...I..."

"...I thought I was yours forever, 'til death did us part..."

"...I do still love you..."

She kicked me again, hard to my kidney.

"Linc, you're a bad guy..." She put her knee on my neck, with pressure to hold it in place. "You used me to help the FBI. Friends of mine died because of it. Their blood is on my hands, and I can't wash it away. No matter how many times you say you love me, you betrayed me. You may have a crazy fixation on me, but I have no pity for you. I think you should be punished..."

"That's crazy talk, Samantha."

"Linc, you were a sweet boy, but you went bad."

I felt the shaft of her gun brush back and forth over my temple. Her knee held my neck firmly to the floor.

"Jesus, Samantha, what are you doing? I can't breathe."

"Linc, you hurt me very much..."

This was not exactly the love-filled reunion I had hoped for.

"Samantha, please let me explain. Everything I've done I've done for you. I went to the Days of Rage because you were there. I worked with the FBI because I thought I might be able to help you, and I did help you. I saved your life. If I hadn't stopped you on West 11th Street when you were walking to the townhouse, you would have been exploded with the rest of them. Please lift your knee. I can't breathe."

"You used me to help the FBI..."

"No, I sacrificed my life for you by trying to tell the true story of what happened at the townhouse. I did that for you, so that you would respect me. I did that for your lost friends. I..."

Big tears poured from my eyes. My chest heaved. I gasped for air.

"Linc, I never asked you to stay in my life. Did it ever cross your mind that you were not wanted? That you were trespassing? That your time with me ended a hundred years ago?"

"Sure. Of course. But you once said you loved me forever, and I thought..."

"Linc, I was seventeen years old."

"Are you alone now? Is there someone in your life?"

"Linc, I'm sorry, but..."

Bang!

I heard the bang, but felt no pain. *So this is how death is*, I thought, surprised I could think so clearly in the after-life. I expected everything to be jumbled and jagged, like an incoherent dream.

Inconsistent with my analysis, however, a team of black clad SWAT guys swarmed into the room. The bang I heard was when they popped open the front door.

Samantha stood up from my neck. She stepped back. "This man broke into my house," she said. "Please arrest him."

The boot of a SWAT guy replaced her knee on my neck, except that for a brief moment in between the changing of the weight I caught a glimpse of her in the whole, a slender sixtyish woman, wearing a blue jogging suit, with salt and pepper hair to her shoulders. I saw through the disguise of her years, saw her as she was on her debutante night. I glowed, and then passed out. I don't remember anything else until I came to my senses strapped to a gurney, immobilized, in a place I didn't know.

"Where am I?" I asked. No one answered.

This took a while to sort out.

I assumed initially that I tripped a wire on my way to the house, which alerted Samantha to draw her weapon, and the Darien police to come quickly to her rescue. But that's not what happened.

Hope got home from her office hours a few minutes after I departed on my mission. I hadn't left a note, or a voice mail, and she wondered where I might have gone so suddenly that I didn't have time to finish my turkey sandwich, which in her experience had not happened before. She snooped around for clues, which she's good at.

My computer still had the MapQuest map and directions on its screen. No time to clean that plate either. She gassed herself up and followed MapQuest's route to Darien. My thought is that she was getting soft on me and thought my itinerary involved some form of two-timing which she needed to get to the bottom of ASAP, and maybe shoot me herself. But she says jealousy was not on her mind. Rather she feared I had jumped aboard a Weatherman wild goose chase and was in danger. Hope is the best.

She eye-balled my car along the shoulder, and tracked my foot-prints back to the perimeter wall, when she heard a gunshot. That would be the warning that Samantha put over my ear. I don't recall giving Fred's cell number to Hope, but she had it, and she called him. She told him she thought I had just been shot in a Weatherman shoot out and gave the address. The SWAT guys were local police, called in by Fred in the interest of speed.

The SWAT guys took me into custody, and promptly turned me over to FBI agents who deposited me in a windowless back room of a private psychiatric hospital, strapped to a gurney, with a guard at the door. As I deconstruct, I probably should not have told Fred about the Weatherman musical featuring my FBI story. Fred did not take this revelation well, as it felt like rocks were being thrown at the windows of an institution he was loyal to, and, worse for me, it sounded to him like I was in serious breach of the confidentiality provisos of my Settlement Agreement, and on my way to making matters a lot worse. I am generally a wise and careful person, as I assume you realize by now, but in my exuberance at being un-blackballed by Liz Caruso I was blind to the prospect of Fred getting on his high horse and reacting with hostility and small-mindedness to my good fortune.

He passed my disclosure of the contemplated musical up the chain of command with a recommendation that the FBI seek to enjoin me from talking and immediately stop my payments. A few hours later when Hope's hysterical call for help came in, he may have recognized an on-going contractual commitment to try to save me from harm, but I think he was more motivated by the new and urgent problem presented by my flapping mouth.

Obviously, Samantha wasn't prosecuted for scaring the shit out of me. Leonard, Hope's ex, her big-time lawyer ex, told me that Samantha likely could have gone ahead and shot me without attracting exposure. "To shoot a stalker who has broken into your house on a dark night in a snowstorm, and is threatening you, whether he's there for old time's sake or otherwise won't likely come back to bite you." Which I will keep in mind if there is a next time.

In fact, Samantha was commended for her calmness and courage in a crisis. She became an instant local hero. I read her interview in the *Darien Times*, which according to my google searches as supplemented by my diligent independent digging over the years was her first public communiqué since she graduated high school. She had lived underground, quietly.

Turns out—as I extrapolate from this published interview—that Samantha married Stan, the guy who was dishonorably and peremptorily discharged from the Weathermen back in December 1969 (at the meeting I attended at Columbia U.). Stan was drafted soon after his discharge (after inadvertently leading the FBI to West 11th Street). He was shot up in 'Nam and returned to America in bandages and on a gurney. Samantha knew him when he was well, and kept a light on for him. She sought him out in his re-hab, where she nursed and nurtured him back to a semblance of his healthy self. He welcomed and embraced her big heart. Love followed, and they shared some happy years, but he still killed himself in 1995, apparently from Vietnam-related reasons (his ghosts refused to die until he did). His family like her family had lots of money, all of which she inherited. She supported the arts and progressive causes, anonymously. She lived reclusively. Forget my musical memoir; I'd like to see hers.

Leonard, Hope's ex. Thank God for Leonard. Hope caught a glimpse of me in the back of the patrol car as they drove me from the scene, and that's the last she saw of me. I was disappeared (again). No paper trail. No recollection at the police station of me being checked in or dropped off *en route*. Fred's cell number rang in space.

For all his reputed failures as a person, Leonard is a finely tuned and fearless litigator, whom you would want to hire and throw your legal fees at when the tiger you've been riding turns to eat you. Leonard, blessed be he, is equipped to stuff that tiger. [Leonard, does that sound about right?]

Hope called him on the morning after I was disappeared and caught him as he was walking into a high stakes, multi-party deposition involving a botched merger, which had many lawyers salivating at the prospect of their anticipated hours. As I understand it, Leonard realized what a shit he was to Hope—dumping her for his young secretary after Hope did nothing but love him truly, acquiesce to his needs and wishes, and raise their children through twenty years of marriage—and so he valued chances to reduce his burden of guilt such as when she asked him for a favor, which she rarely did because she thought he deserved to stay on the hook and bleed.

She described the situation tearfully to Leonard—"Leonard, I don't know where he is. I don't know what they've done with him. Nobody's talking..." Leonard listened patiently while a battle line of hard-boiled litigators with thousands of dollars in aggregate hourly fees sat quietly and fiddled with their paper clips as it became known that he was taking a call from his ex, a situation universally recognized for its extreme volatility, and meriting professional courtesy regardless of age, gender, sexual orientation, current marital status or client considerations.

"Okay," Leonard said to Hope, "I'm on the case."

To his bag-carrying junior associate he said, "Sue, you're at bat. Don't fuck up."

He exited the deposition.

My disappearance was a red meat redemptive opportunity for him. "Don't worry about the fee," Hope told me later. "Leonard owes me big time."

By three o'clock that afternoon Leonard was standing before a United States District Court judge with a petition for *habeas corpus*, demanding that the United States account for my body, which at the time was still MIA.

He caught the government flat-footed. An Assistant U.S. Attorney—Marv Dungerman—rushed to the hearing on short notice to say that he didn't know who I was or where I was but would look into it. The judge ordered Dungerman to find me and produce me in court within twenty-four hours.

Dungerman found me, but didn't produce me. "Your honor," he said when the hearing re-convened on the afternoon of the next day, "Mr. Cox is in a psychiatric ward, undergoing tests. It is not feasible to move him at this time."

"Bring him to this court," the judge said.

"Further, your honor," Dungerman continued, "I am informed that Mr. Cox poses a clear and imminent threat to national security in that he has information which he intends to release which if released will do serious and substantial harm and damage to the United States..."

"What's that information?" asked the judge.

"I can't tell you," said Dungerman, "because it is in the nature of a state secret."

"How do you know he intends to release it?" asked the judge.

"I can't tell you," said Dungerman, "because it is in the nature of a state secret."

"Where is he?" asked the judge.

"I can't tell you," said Dungerman, "because it is in the nature of a state secret."

The judge was pissed. Leonard too. Leonard urged the judge to hold Dungerman in contempt. And lock him up.

Dungerman blinked at that. "Your honor," he said, "I have my son's basketball game tonight."

"Mr. Dungerman," the judge said, "I know of no basis in law to hold an American citizen in secret detention, away from the purview of the courts of the United States. You will produce Mr. Cox in one hour or answer to the consequences."

I'm going by the transcript. I wish I had been there. This is how one must feel when due to circumstances beyond one's control one misses one's own funeral but gets to read the eulogy.

I was produced. It took two hours, but the judge allowed the extra time after Dungerman begged for it, saying I was on the way but stuck in traffic. I walked into court looking like a mangy beast, in the same clothes I wore for stalking. My trusty tweed was nearly dead, and in fact was pronounced dead a week later on a dry cleaner's board when efforts to revive him failed and I elected to convert his frayed remnants into a wall hanging. My frizzy beard was gone to seed, in the style favored by homeless wanderers. I was unwashed and odiferous. Hope hugged me, metaphorically. Leonard shook my hand, and discreetly wiped my cooties off on Hope's coat.

A thicket of legal wrangling ensued, centered around where I was going to stay that night. Dungerman, now backed by a team of eager-beaver-looking Justice Department lawyers, argued to the judge that I should stay in Federal custody pending arraignment on charges of violation of the Espionage Act, and a bail hearing, and failing that I should be sent back to Darien, Connecticut to face state criminal charges of stalking, breaking and entering, and criminal trespass. Leonard argued that the government had abused me, could not be trusted to have custody of me, that the Espionage Act charges against me were illusory, trumped-up, without merit, and an affront to established principles of justice, that the state law charges were motivated by malice, that I wasn't about to blab anything to anybody, and that I should be released on personal recognizance forthwith.

The judge, fortunately, was still pissed.

"Mr. Durango," the judge said to Leonard, "if I order that Mr. Cox be released into your custody for the night, will you accept that duty, and see that he takes a shower, gets a night's sleep, and returns to this court tomorrow morning at ten o'clock for an evidentiary hearing on the risk, if any, he poses to the United States?"

"I will, your honor."

One of the new Justice Department lawyers jumped up. "Your honor," he said, "Brian J. Looper for the United States, may it please the court, if you release Mr. Cox from federal custody for the night, he will be free and able to tell the world the state secrets which we seek to prevent him from telling."

"You're saying there is a real likelihood of that happening, Mr. Looper?"

"Yes, your honor."

"And the risk is so great that we can't wait for a hearing tomorrow morning?"

"That's correct, your honor."

"Even if I order Mr. Cox to not reveal anything until then?"

"Yes, your honor."

"Then I release Mr. Durango from the responsibility of custody over Mr. Cox, and I appoint you, Mr. Looper, to have custody over Mr. Cox for the night, at a three star or better hotel of your choosing, and see that he gets a shower, a meal, a night's sleep, a change of clothes, and returns to this court tomorrow morning at ten o'clock for an evidentiary hearing."

Looper looked deflated, like he was close to saying something like, "Your honor, that was bull shit I was feeding you about Cox posing an imminent risk. I was just trying to harass him a little more to improve our negotiating posture. So let's leave him with Mr. Durango for the night, and I'll see him and you back here tomorrow morning ..." But instead with a sour face he said, "Thank you, your honor. I will be pleased to take custody of Mr. Cox."

Before being escorted to my hotel room, I had a moment with Leonard and Hope, who (whom?) were aglow from their day's work and were finishing each other's sentences. Which was a good sign, in that some exes would have committed double murder suicides by now on account of the renewed pressure and proximity.

✱

THE NEXT MORNING'S HEARING TOOK MORE UNEXPECTED TURNS. Dungerman and Looper sat in the audience, not at the counsel table. The United States had a new lead attorney, Herman Gout, a natty older gent, "seasoned" is the word they sometimes apply to his type, although "wily" works for me. Herman started by apologizing to the judge for all the confusion of the last couple days, effectively throwing Dungerman and Looper under the wheel of justice. Herman also offered a heartfelt apology to me for all my discomfort, if and to the extent I was or may have been wrongfully discomforted.

"Your honor," he said to the judge, not to me, "it has taken us a bit of time to get up to speed, to get a handle on the issues involving Mr. Cox. But now I am pleased to report that we have it..."

"What is it?" asked the judge.

"We are not pressing Federal criminal charges against Mr. Cox..."

Good news.

"No Espionage Act? No criminal conspiracies?" the judge asked.

"Correct. Although I do not speak for the State of Connecticut, and the state law criminal claims of stalking, criminal trespass, and breaking and entering, which are pending against him in state court..."

Not such good news.

"So, our work here is done?" asked the judge.

"Yes and no, your honor. Yes, in that we're not charging Mr. Cox with federal crimes. Yes, in that we don't seek custody or incarceration of him. But no, in that we have this morning filed a civil complaint with this court against Mr. Cox arising from his breaches and anticipatory breaches of his Settlement Agreement with the FBI."

Uh oh. A rabbit from his hat.

Old Gout handed papers to the judge's clerk, who handed them up to the judge. Gout handed a similarly thick stack to Leonard, who cast an evil eye upon them.

Gout continued: "As you will see, your honor, the Settlement Agreement—a true copy of which is attached as Exhibit A—prohibits Mr. Cox from revealing in any way the non-public relationship he had with the FBI in the calendar years 1969 and 1970, and thereafter. We allege that Mr. Cox has breached this prohibition, in substantial and material ways, and threatens to further breach this prohibition, causing and threatening substantial harm and damage to the FBI, to the United States, and to the American people. We seek injunctive relief enjoining Mr. Cox from revealing information in breach of his Settlement Agreement. And in connection therewith, we seek an order releasing the FBI of and from any and all further payment obligations due Mr. Cox under his Settlement Agreement, together with damages in the form of disgorgement of all monies heretofore paid to Mr. Cox under the Settlement Agreement, plus costs, interest, and attorney fees. And may it please the court, we seek a hearing on our request for a preliminary injunction against Mr. Cox, said hearing to commence forthwith before you, said hearing to be closed to the public and the transcript sealed ..."

I felt like a soccer ball getting the shit kicked out of me/it, or a tennis ball reduced to fetch games with a salivating dog, or a ping pong ball squashed flat by a semi, or a golf ball landed in a fetid water hazard, or a....

"Mr. Durango?" asked the judge.

"One moment please," Leonard said. He leaned over to Hope in the seat next to him and engaged in an animated tete a tete with her, each whispering into the other's ear at a mile a minute. I tried to make it a three way from my seat on the far side of Hope, but all their ears and tongues were engaged. Which was probably good, because the only contribution I had to make on the subject of the FBI not paying me my $200,000 bonus and otherwise threatening to re-arrange with extreme prejudice my retirement plan, was to moan.

Our team decided to play it as it lay. Leonard rose to welcome the challenge. "Your honor," he said, "the non-disclosure components of the Settlement Agreement which the United States seeks to enforce were obtained through duress, coercion and illegality, and are not enforceable as a matter of law. The request of the United States for preliminary injunctive relief must be denied..."

As Leonard went on to outline my defenses and counterclaims, apparently I had many of them, Hope whispered to me, "Linc, don't worry. We anticipated this. We prepared all night." Again, a good thing that Leonard and Hope were so harmonic in my defense.

If you are the plaintiff in a preliminary injunction hearing, which is in effect a pre-trial trial, your goal is to freeze things in place until the real trial. The deal for you is to establish that it is *likely* you will win on the merits at the real trial, i.e., that you will prove your case, and that you can't wait the year or two years or whenever until the real trial to get relief because you will suffer "irreparable harm and damage" if you have to wait without relief. On the other hand, if you are a defendant—such as myself—in a preliminary injunction hearing, the deal is to puncture wounds in the plaintiff's evidence, and also to show that plaintiff has acted in bad faith, with dishonesty, duplicity, mean-spiritedness and the like. The technical term is "unclean hands." Somewhere in the dusty annals of Anglo-American jurisprudence it became axiomatic that the plaintiff has to be pure of heart and deed, i.e., have clean hands, to be entitled to the relief of a preliminary injunction. [My source for this legal info is Leonard, as he told it to Hope, as she packaged it for me, as I drank my Scotch.]

We proceeded on a hearing on preliminary injunction. Then and there. Behind closed courtroom doors. Justice on a fast and closed-to-the-public track.

"I call Dr. Eric Feather as my first witness," Old Gout said. *Huh, Dr. Feather?* I looked around the courtroom, *not there, not there, not there, yes there he is in the back of the room.* Dr. F in the flesh, walking forward to the witness stand. He wore a dark blue suit, a white shirt, a conservative tie. He looked subdued, dignified and confident. Even his outsize nose looked subdued, dignified and confident. He was sworn in.

"Do you swear to tell the truth, the whole truth and nothing but the truth so help you God?"

"I do."

"Please state your name."

"Eric Feather."

"Are you employed?"

"I am self-employed, as a board-certified psychiatrist."

"Are you testifying today pursuant to a subpoena?"

"Yes, I am."

"Which means what to you?"

"It means that I am testifying because the court is ordering me to testify, not because I voluntarily want to dump shit on Mr. Cox." [That's what I heard, arguably not what he said.].

"Are you familiar with an organization called the Weathermen?"

"Yes, I am."

"What is it?"

"Today it's just a memory, but back in the late Sixties and early Seventies it was an organization of people, mostly under thirty years old, whose common goal was to stop the War in Vietnam."

"Is it fair to call the Weathermen a 'radical' organization?"

"I guess it was left of mainstream back in the Sixties, but I think the righteousness of its opposition to the War is now generally accepted."

"Generally?"

"Widely."

"Are you now or have you ever been a member of the Weatherman organization?"

"I was a member for about a year, ending in March 1970."

"Why did you cease being a member?"

"A few reasons, but mostly because elements of the Weathermen were proselytizing a bombing agenda which I didn't agree with. I sympathized with their frustration as more and more people were killed in the senseless war, but I did not want to associate myself with domestic bombing."

"Do you know an individual whose name is Lincoln Cox?"

"Yes, I do."

He pointed me out. I raised my hand.

"Have you had discussions with him recently?"

"Yes, I have."

"Where and when?"

"In a Starbucks on the Upper West Side, and in my office also on the Upper West Side, within the last few days.

"In those discussions did Mr. Cox affirmatively state that during March 1970, he was an undercover agent for the FBI?"

"Yes, he did."

"In those discussions did Mr. Cox describe his work as an undercover agent for the FBI?"

"Yes, he did."

"What did he say?"

"He said his work for the FBI was to infiltrate the Weatherman organization, under the guise of being a reporter."

"Did he say whether he was successful in this infiltration?"

"Yes, he said he successfully infiltrated a Weatherman cell located in a townhouse at 18 West 11th Street, Greenwich Village, Manhattan, on or about March 5, 1970, and that he passed along his observations to the FBI."

"That's 18 West 11th Street?

"Yes, sir."

"Prior to your discussions with Mr. Cox, were you aware of FBI efforts to infiltrate this Weathermen cell?"

"No, I was not."

"Thank you, Dr. Feather." Turning to the judge, old Gout said, "I have no further questions of this witness at this time." He walked to his seat, wearing a smug smile like he had done the deed, i.e., he had elicited testimony to the effect that I was spilling the FBI's beans.

"Your witness, Mr. Durango," said the judge.

Leonard Durango rose to face Dr. F, who sat with apparent calm and suavity in his witness chair, and the hint of a knowing and smug smile as I interpreted it. "Thank you, your honor."

Leonard began with a slow, seemingly direction-free stroll through the factoids of Dr. Feather's life, asking about his schools, parents, degrees, training, publications, marriages, divorces, malpractice claims, medical board disciplinary charges, gambling debts, DWI arrests and the like, as though he was on a fishing expedition, just worming up his hook and hoping to get lucky.

And he got surprisingly lucky, making me think he had a fish finding gizmo up his sleeve. Small fry mostly, but enough to put Dr. F in a discomfort zone. Sweat beads pearled on his forehead. He swatted imaginary flies. I wouldn't have guessed, for example, that his first wife hammered his nose into its current bulbous configuration with a cast iron frying pan.

Leonard was smooth as silk. No notes. No arguments with the witness. No pauses. Just a flow of cool question after cool question after cool question, until this one, "Dr. Feather, are you being paid by the United States government for your testimony this morning?"

"Of course not."

"Have you ever been paid by the United States government for any services?"

"For testifying?"

"Any services, not just for testifying."

"No, I...well, what are you getting at?"

"Any services."

"You mean like medical services?"

"Not just medical services."

"You mean like in the past five or so years?"

"Ever, from the beginning of time."

"Well, I...it's sort of a broad question..."

Leonard raised his palm to Dr. F, like a traffic cop at an intersection to a driver trying to slide by on the fringe. As if to say, "Stop. You won't get away with that shit with me."

And to the judge Leonard said, "Excuse me, your honor, may I have a moment to speak with my client?"

"Yes."

Dr. F stayed in his witness seat, clearly not knowing which way this was going, dabbing sweat drops.

Leonard approached Hope and me. We huddled up. "Linc," Hope whispered, "this is very important. Think back to Thursday morning, March 5, 1970, when you saw two sticks of dynamite in a waste basket in the townhouse hallway. Did you really see two sticks of dynamite?"

"I..."

"Or did you see two tall cups of Coke with straws?"

"I...I told the FBI that I saw dynamite."

"But was it?"

"They wanted me to find dynamite."

"But was it?"

"It was a long time ago..."

"That's what I thought," Hope whispered. To Leonard she said, "Let's go for it."

"Go for what?" I asked.

Leonard blew Hope a half kiss, and me the other half, as we broke huddle and he re-approached the witness. "Dr. Feather," he said, "have you ever been paid by the United States government for any services?"

"Again, Mr. Durango, could you narrow that down?"

"Fine, Dr. Feather. I'll do just that. Have you ever been paid as an informer by the FBI?"

Dr. F did a double take, a double double take. "Are you crazy? Are you accusing me? What are you saying?"

"Please answer my question, Dr. Feather. Have you ever been paid as an informer by the FBI?"

"No, of course not."

"You are under oath, Dr. Feather. It's a criminal offense to lie under oath. I will ask you one more time. Are you now or have you ever been paid as an informer by the FBI?"

"What do you mean by 'informer'"?

"The common meaning of the word, Dr. Feather. Snitch, rat, mole, stooge, fink, collaborator. Dr. Feather, have you ever been paid as an informer by the FBI?"

"What do you mean by..." He paused mid-sentence. "I don't know what you mean..." His strong self seemed to leave his body at that moment, like life at the onset of death. He sagged.

"March 1970," Leonard said, "Greenwich Village townhouse at 18 West 11th Street. Paid to inform on the Weathermen?"

Dr. F mouthed the word, "No," then changed to "Yes."

I felt sorry for him. One minute he's leisurely swimming around his peaceful pond, and the next minute he's in the frying pan getting cooked for dinner. One minute he is a man of parts and dignity, a man of accomplishment and principle, and the next minute his lifelong secret is exposed, and all the rest of him no longer counts.

But on the other hand, screw him. Why should I feel sorry for him? He didn't feel sorry for me. He didn't do five years of hard(ish) time on account of trying to do the right thing. He went to med school, and started his lucrative career. He wasn't despised by Samantha. He was her guru, and for all I knew more.

After the horse had left the barn—as we say up here in horse country, where I am now ensconced, in Leonard's country home, preparing for trial—after F fell and cracked his shell and was not about to be put back together again, old Gout rose to object to Leonard's line of questions. "He's badgering the witness, your honor."

"Goes to the truthfulness of the witness," Leonard said to the judge. "Impeaches his testimony on direct...And your honor, goes to the 'clean hands' of the United States. Their hands are dirtier than you know what..."

✳

ON BREAK, after the EMTs wheeled F out of the courtroom, I asked Hope and Leonard how they happened to get the idea that he—not unlike myself—was a rat. "Did you just have a hunch that you ran with?"

Their eyes met, and they smiled at each other, twinkled is a closer description. "Linc, honey," Hope said, "of course we think the FBI had a predilection to infiltrate in depth, with compartmentalized resources, so that it was unlikely you were the only one. But we didn't finger F until last night..."

"What happened last night?"

Another twinkle. Hope touched me on the hand. "Linc, you reported to the FBI that you saw two sticks of dynamite in a bucket?"

"Yes."

"Did you really?"

"Well...I saw what I saw. I saw the situation..."

"Because, viewed by the light of day, it sounded to me like you were hallucinating..."

"Or dissembling," Leonard added.

"But..." I mildly protested.

"The FBI," Hope said, "needed dynamite to get their green light. You reported dynamite..."

"I wanted to do the right thing."

"I see that," Hope said, "and I'm not judging you..." She raised an eyebrow in the direction of Leonard. He eyebrowed her back. They seemed to be sipping from the same can of soda.

"Why didn't you ask me about the dynamite before?" I asked.

"I didn't put two and two together until we started preparing for Feather's testimony last night. I walked through what he said to us about..."

"...why the Weathermen were having a meeting?"

"...Exactly. He said he was coming down from New Haven for a meeting at the townhouse about the bombing plans, and was worried in the first place that they would blow themselves up by getting sloppy with the explosives. He said some moron had left two sticks of dynamite in a basket..."

"...I get it..."

"...Correct. If sticks weren't in the basket, then who could have told Feather that they were?"

"...Only the FBI..."

"...You told them, they passed it to Feather, he adopted it. The Weathermen weren't going to tell Feather such a story, to say to him that they were sloppy fools with the dynamite. If they realized they were sloppy with the dynamite, they would have stopped being sloppy."

"...Okay. Maybe. So are you saying the FBI told him about the sticks because they wanted him to go down to the townhouse to put the sticks in a safe place, to save the Weathermen from blowing themselves up from their sloppiness?"

"...That's more than I'm saying..."

"...Then are you saying that he got the idea on his own to save the Weathermen from their sloppiness? That he was really a hero in sheep's clothing? Or given a couple more hours and a faster train from New Haven, could have been a hero..."

"...I don't see any heroes in this episode," Hope said.

"...I tried to be a hero to Samantha," I said.

We all three nodded, but I don't know if we all three were nodding for the same reasons. History gets confusing.

✳

DRAGGING DR. F DOWN FELT GOOD BUT DIDN'T EXACTLY EXON-
ERATE ME. At the end of the day the judge ordered me not to talk
about my FBI experiences, and to put my rock musical in the holding
pen, pending trial which he scheduled to begin in ninety days. He put
off disposition of money claims until then.

"Linc," Leonard said, "we have some work to do if we're going
to keep you out of jail in Connecticut, and keep your FBI settlement
money flowing. I want you to write down your whole story, hold
nothing back, and deliver it to me ASAP..."

So that's what I'm doing.

In Leonard's big country house, a converted farmhouse. I'm the
only one in it.

It's in the middle of woods and fields, a half-mile from the nearest
person. The internet connection comes and goes. Ditto with my cell
phone.

The dirt road to town was impassable today because of a late
winter blizzard.

At night I hear coyotes howl.

I don't mind that Hope and Leonard are back together.

Leonard is negotiating with Samantha's attorney, to have her
drop charges. No progress to date. She thinks I'll keep stalking her
if I'm free. Could be. Driving to her house in Darien speaks for itself,
doesn't it?

Incidentally, I'm pretty sure it was Samantha who put F up to
calling Liz Seaver Caruso last winter in Boston, to blackball me.
Samantha got wind of my book plans, and saw me heading in her
direction, and that forced her out of reclusion. Which I think was
probably good for her, to get her back into the flow of things, not that
I expect her to thank me any time soon.

F moved to a spiritual community in the Rocky Mountains. Hope
thinks it's a load off his mind that he's been outed. Maybe, but I
doubt it.

Hope was very helpful in getting me a paid leave of absence from
school. A couple of my students sent me get well notes, along with

their requests for references for their law school applications.

Leonard says that if we could convince the United States that I will not blow the FBI's cover on the townhouse explosion, they will back off on the money claims. And maybe sweeten the pot. Something to think about. Arguably a happy ending, because the fact is I'm ready to retire from the exposure business. I'm too old for it. It's gotten me into too much trouble. I don't see it winning me any points with Samantha, and besides, I can use the cash.

From now on my motto is to let sleeping dogs lie. If the FBI felt the need to slap down the Weathermen, maybe the FBI knew something. If I did work for the FBI, maybe that was the patriotic thing to do.

The Vietnam War? The lesson I take from it is that no matter how urgent the immediate ideological problem, don't get involved.

AFTERWORD

EXCEPT MY LIFE WENT ON.

I handed-in the above pages to Leonard and Hope. We had a hand-in meeting at Leonard's high-rise office at Madison and 50th. Very swank. The potted plants are groomed daily and look prosperous. The young women wear the high heels and click-clack on the marble floors. The aerial views were formerly reserved for God.

Leonard was flanked by girl and boy associates, eager to please. They addressed me as Professor Cox, the esteemed client (i.e., in the legal culture/business, all clients are treated as esteemed, without regard to the stink that may waft around them and their cases, mostly). They salivated at the chance to probe my thick memoir for exonerating factoids. I felt like a chicken pot pie. Hope looked good, for her age group, as she always does. Everything organized and in place, with a discreet sensuality, eyelids slightly heavy, breasts pushing gently against their confinement, gold that dangled. I perceived a bloom to her oasis.

They brought lunch to our conference room. Gourmet sandwiches and chips, with a nice selection of soda and water products. The servers—who wheeled in the food cart and set up the spread on the credenza—wore snappy green aprons, embossed with the firm logo. The whole mission was clean, timely, served with a smile, and damn tasty. I don't know if I could work in a corporate law office all day every day (not that anyone is asking), but I definitely could eat lunch there.

The big news was that Leonard, Hope and Hillary—Hillary being Leonard's former secretary and current wife, and in her third trimester with Leonard's child—are working out their rules for a live-together lifestyle. If I were to tell Hope what I really thought, I'd tell her that her role had "nanny" written all over it, but she obviously doesn't see it that way. She's blooming, like she's the one who's pregnant. Or like she knows something Hillary doesn't. I don't ask about sleeping arrangements.

I wish her only well. Do I sound hurt and jealous?

I assume Leonard knows his way around a pre-nup, and probably around a pre-nup à trois as well.

I pressed Leonard for progress on the Samantha front.

"She won't talk to you."

"What if we structured an in-person mediation with lots of safeguards..."

"You didn't hear me. She won't talk to you."

"What if I show up at her house in broad daylight, very contrite, with my hat in my hand..."

"You would be trespassing, and in violation of court orders, and her security people might shoot you."

"Seriously, I really want to see her..."

"Linc," Leonard said to me, leaning close so as not to be overheard, and with his words naturally camouflaged by chomping and slurping sounds, "your wish to see her presents psychiatric issues that I as your lawyer do not have an answer for."

"So, are you saying that I should not try to see her..."

"...Yes, that's exactly what I'm saying..."

"...or that I probably should not try to see her..."

"...No, that's not what I'm saying."

"...or that if I try to see her I should expect the worst, but that maybe things will work out as they sometimes do in these circumstances..."

"...No, not that at all."

Leonard was a downer, a big dose of negativity, a burst of cold rain. Too much lawyer and not enough dreamer for my taste. From a reverse engineering standpoint on the subject of Samantha, he was trying to re-invent the wheel after the horse had left the barn, if you can visualize what I mean. I was a committed horse, and on the loose.

I exited Leonard's building, stuffed and blue. The work that had kept me busy and engaged for more than a month was done and out of my hands. Where to go from here I didn't know. At just that moment, however, as the circling door delivered me to the street, the cloudbank that had sat on top of Manhattan for a week— dripping cold drizzle on baseball fans, seeping into arthritic joints at every income level, threatening never to leave—picked itself up and blew away, and was replaced by bright, soothing April sunshine. I took that as a sign.

A sign that my time with Samantha would come, if I was patient and persevering enough. Arguably other people might have taken different signs from the cloud dispersal. I wish them success with their different signs, it being a free country, without legal restrictions on what signs one can take from random meteorological events.

The sunshine was short-lived. The cloudbank re-formed with greater grayness and density before the hour was over, and it started to rain. I was soaked to the bone when I emerged from a trance-like state of mind, standing across the street from 18 West 11th.

The ring on my cell phone emerged me.

It was Hope.

"Linc, where are you?"

"I'm on the street."

"Are you okay?"

"I'm fine."

"I didn't like the way you left Leonard's office."

"I'm fine."

"Leonard thinks you're going to visit Samantha."

"No, not at all."

"That would be really stupid and self-destructive."

"I wouldn't do that. Don't worry. *Achooo.*"

"Where are you?"

They built a new townhouse on the site of the explosion. It's red brick, but with modern design features. An impressive structure. Beaming and attractive. The rest of the street looked about the same as it did the last time I was there, on the far side of the Gulf of Time, when sirens screamed and lurid flames shot into the air.

Those were the days. Bad days.

"I appreciate that you care about me, Hope. I do. You are wonderful."

"I don't think you're doing well."

"That's probably true."

I contemplated telling Hope that I thought she was a fool to engage with Hillary and Leonard, and their soon-to-be baby. But that's not what she wanted to hear, and I doubted I could change her course anyway. What good would it do to agitate? She likely felt the same about me and mine.

"Linc," she said, "call me." She let me go.

That night I caught a break.

Or arguably I earned it, by diligently tracking google leads until my fingers hurt I googled out that the Town of Brookline, Massachusetts, Samantha's home town—site of her family manse, wherefrom I was dragooned back in the day—was naming a park after Samantha's late mother, who to her dying day blamed me for everything bad that Samantha stepped in. In a roundabout way, however, I think she was ok with me. I could absorb abuse. I didn't hit back. I had the lifelong blessing of Harvard admissions.

I leapt to the conclusion that Samantha's hand was on the checkbook for the making of this commemorative park event, and that she would be there in the flesh for the opening. In my experience they don't kick you out of a funeral no matter how much the survivors detest you because, what the hell, the deceased might have viewed you more favorably, might have welcomed your sympathies despite years of publicly displayed antipathy. The event is all about the deceased. *Tomorrow you should not set foot within my sight, but for today you have a pass.* I assumed the same might apply to a park-naming ceremony, notwithstanding court orders to the contrary.

The park was a modern little thing, concrete shapes that worked both as art and jungle gyms, young shrubs trying their best to get acclimated, benches for moms and lovers, a festoon of early-in-the season tulips. It was converted from a vacant lot, sandwiched between low-rise buildings in the commercial part of town, near the post office where you may recall I posted my exposé—having walked down the hill from the Victor manse, imbued with youthful bees in my bonnet, too late in the day to find a working copy machine, distrustful of the politics of the postal clerk who viewed my package with the suspicion of a person on the short hair side of the culture war—which was seized by the FBI from the grasp of my newspaper editor, and removed from circulation with extreme prejudice. Reflecting on these old events, encrusted as they are by the scab of time, gets me thinking on whether too much picking is a smart thing to do, and if so, how does one stop?

I arrived at the park site at 1:00 PM on the Saturday of the ceremony, an hour early. I'd taken a bus up from Connecticut, where I'd been passing slow time, waiting for my trial. Back in my apartment having been uninvited by Hillary (with the apparent assent of Leonard and Hope) from further extending my stay at Leonard's country house after I handed in my assignment, not that I miss the scare tactics of the local coyotes. I wore a disguise to the park. Dark glasses. Baseball cap pulled low. Pea jacket collar pulled high. Unidentifiable in a line-up, even by myself.

A cloudless sky with no rain was forecast, which is a good sign for any outdoor event, except maybe a family picnic you hope will be cancelled, or a horse race when you've bet the mudder. Temperature in the low 60s. A light breeze with a few molecules of balminess drifting up from Bermuda. The earth, to the extent unpaved, breathed after its winter slumber, exuding a rich and loamy scent like it'd been wanded by the Goddess of Fertility.

I felt like the earth. My day was all about re-birth and second chances. And if possible, don't get arrested. A green table was set up in the center of the park, ahead of rows of folding chairs, enough to accommodate a sitting crowd in the mid-twenties. A worker worked on the electronics.

"Testing, 1-2-3. Testing, 1-2-3."

The sound system seemed to be working.

The seats began to fill, many with high-end dowager types, contemporaries of the honoree. I imagined a few of these had last seen me as a young man, in the back seat of an FBI car, being whisked from the Victor estate in the dead of night, my plan to expose the FBI DOA, likewise my plan for my life. *Hello witnesses*, I jokingly murmured to myself.

Dignitaries milled around the green table, one of them religiously collared, another holding the proclamation, a third dressed like a firefighter. I drifted to a post against a concrete donut, near the back, off to the side for good sight lines, nearly invisible, which is how and where I am comfortable at a funeral or its thematic equivalent.

A television camera crew arrived. *The whole world is watching*, I jokingly murmured to myself. I was full of joking murmurs to myself. They were bleating out of me like gas after a bowl of cabbage. Two guys sat still and respectfully on a bench on the far side, wearing trench coats and thick, black, rubber-soled shoes. Had to be FBI. Had to be. *Plus ca change...*

There was commotion on the sidewalk. A hug cluster was forming, four joined by two more spilling out of a vintage VW bus, clad in beads and psychedelia, aged versions of Alan Ginsburg, Mary Travers, and George Harrison, along with Tim from the Casablanca Bar who was a contender for the underground longevity crown. Here for Samantha. I was touched by the tribute, and by the memories these oldies provoked.

And across the street at the tailgate of a minivan the head of a counter cluster was handing out placards and American flags to persons who looked to be clean-cut, law-abiding, God-fearing, tunnel-visioned crackpots. Also here for Samantha. I assumed they were on somebody's payroll.

The placards were blunt spoken. "Weathermen are Terrorists. Don't Forgive. Don't Forget." When every crackpot had a poster, and/or flag, they began to chant the words: "Weathermen are Terrorists. Don't Forgive. Don't Forget."

I pulled my cap down another notch, for greater invisibility.

Samantha appeared at the gate. Bride-like. Her salt and pepper hair was woven into a single braid that dangled down her back. Her posture was debutante perfect. Her stride was fluid, and with each stride the train of her long black coat swayed within a thread of the ground. She carried blood red roses. I gasped for air, for all the old reasons, and for some new ones thrown in.

She was unescorted.

She reached the green table, was greeted by the dignitaries, and by some of the old crows, and set herself in the first row with her roses.

Chanting from the street continued. "Weathermen are terrorists. Don't forgive. Don't forget."

Answered once or twice by a counter chant: "Forgive. Forget. Fuck You."

The cleric blessed us all and requested a few moments of silence from the chanticleers. "Come inside our tent, and rest your placards," he urged them. They grumbled, but miraculously the cleric had his way. The pros and the cons entered the park, pushing and shoving each other for better site lines.

The cleric thanked them for resting their chants and continued. "Annette Victor was, by all accounts, a brilliant, beautiful, accomplished and resilient woman, who dedicated her life to good deeds, not the least of which was her support for the public parks of Brookline. It is a welcome and fitting tribute to her that we should open this lovely park, on this lovely spring day, in her name..."

The chief politician in attendance read the proclamation, ending with the words, "and I am pleased to present this proclamation to Samantha Victor, daughter of Annette Victor, and daughter of Brookline, Massachusetts, with our heartfelt appreciation for her generosity..."

Samantha rose, and accepted the proclamation with a firm hand-shake, and a luminous smile.

The chief politician asked if she would say a few words.

She paused, and I didn't know which way she would go. She

scanned the crowd, making sense of who was there and why. Her eyes didn't linger when they reached me—up against my concrete donut—which pleased the good angels in my head who wanted to avoid a scene, but not the banana-brained bad ones who dreamt of a reality-bending happy ending.

"Thank you, Reverend," Samantha said. "I think my mother would be very happy with this park..."

This was too much nice talk for the cons. They burst into their chant. "Weathermen are terrorists. Don't forgive. Don't forget." They started to march on Samantha.

The pros took immediate offense and blocked the cons' path. Shoving commenced. Chants turned to screams. A melee burst out, except one rogue con escaped from the pack and darted to the front, waving his placard like a knight in shining armor, taking direct aim at Samantha. I remember leaving my post, running to a point of interception, and diving into the erstwhile attacker, but I don't remember after that.

I opened my eyes in a hospital bed.

I could move my arms freely and wasn't cuffed to the bed frame. Which was good news, because I've been cuffed to bed frames before. My neck, however, was in a brace. I could only see above me, and not around.

"You have a cracked head."

Who was talking to me? Who was this nurturing voice?

"You took twelve stitches above your eye. You have a concussion, and a broken nose..."

"Samantha?" I asked.

"No, I'm Elaine, your nurse."

Of course. Elaine. What dream was I living?

She bustled away.

"I'm Samantha," another voice said, surprising me from the far side of the room.

THE END

ACKNOWLEDGEMENTS

FIRST ACKNOWLEDGEMENT

I could argue that the disillusionment and advocacy of violence of the Weathermen 50 years ago compares (as I observe the news) to feelings held by some untethered militants today, as well as to many other disenfranchised and disoriented tribes through history. An injustice needs to be stopped, nothing else matters. "I pledge to the cause, I sacrifice my life, I waive the succor of normalcy."

This thought makes me very unhappy. I wish for informed discussion and compromise of grievances, for salve on burning wounds, for a path to healing and harmony. In these respects I am, I acknowledge, a fool. A member of my own crackpot tribe of reality distortionists. "The arc of the moral universe is long, but it bends toward justice...," sayeth Barack Obama, echoing Martin Luther King, Jr. But with deep regret, and as good as it sounds, I am resistant. I assume that the germ of evil shall not perish from the earth.

While my story is in large part a romp, a picaresque, a jape, a conspiracy theory, a tale of quixotic love, I acknowledge that blood was shed in the wings of the love story, that the background scenery is not harmless or fun, that the Vietnam War was a terrible disaster and miscalculation, and that the idea of bringing it home was also a terrible disaster and miscalculation. There is no joy in telling this part.

SECOND ACKNOWLEDGEMENT

I acknowledge, posthumously, JS. He was a friend who died way too young. I do not purport to be qualified to tell his story. He was a friend, but I barely knew him. I remember that he was unafraid to flaunt convention, unafraid to run his own path, and a bright star worthy of remembrance and esteem. The vines of time curl around his memory and threaten to absorb him into the past. To which I object, and hereby unhinge my vine clipper.

THIRD ACKNOWLEDGEMENT

I acknowledge (and thank) NLC for finding and exhuming my manuscript from a forgotten crypt in the basement of my computer. She read aloud, and we laughed. She breathed life into my story.

FOURTH ACKNOWLEDGEMENT

Thank you, ER (some are silver, you are gold). Also, thanks to my everyday starting line-up: ACL, ZJC, GL, CC, I, B, Z, and C, with a shout out to GP/KP (honorary members). A lifetime achievement award to RJ/SS. A bravo to KS for thoughtful support. A bouquet to LV for production and design.

FIFTH ACKNOWLEDGEMENT

Those vines of time. Like AML, impervious (except that when I close my eyes we are still alive and we dance).

—JDC

ABOUT THE AUTHOR

JONATHAN CANTER IS A RETIRED ATTORNEY; widower; devoted father and grandfather (sounds like my obit); lifelong resident of Greater Boston; graduate of Harvard College (where he was an editor *The Harvard Lampoon*); lover of the ocean (as seen from the shore); sporadic writer of dry and sometimes dark humor (see *Lucky Leonardo* (Sourcebooks, 2004), funny to the edge of tears); gamesman (see *A Crapshooter's Companion*, ISBN 978-1-7923-1003-4 (2019), existential thriller and life manual); and student of the late '60s.

Made in the USA
Monee, IL
08 January 2021